HELLO KITTY®
Surprise!

stories and art by
Jacob Chabot, Ian McGinty
and Jorge Monlongo

hello kitty shorts by
Anastassia Neislotova

HELLO KITTY

Surprise!

Stories and Art Jacob Chabot, Ian McGinty, Jorge Monlongo
Endpapers and Shorts Anastassia Neislotova

Cover Art Jacob Chabot
Cover and Book Design Shawn Carrico
Editor Traci N. Todd

Printed in China

Published by VIZ Media, LLC
P.O. Box 77010
San Francisco, CA 94107

10 9 8 7 6 5 4 3 2 1
First printing, April 2014

"Fintastic Day at the Beach," "Treasure!," "Ghost Story," and "To the Rescue"
Stories and art by Ian McGinty, colors by Papillon Studios

"The Egg" and "Party Time"
Stories and art by Jorge Monlongo

"Up"
Story by Traci N. Todd and Jacob Chabot, art by Jacob Chabot

"About Time," "Masked Ball," and "Surprise!"
Stories by Traci N. Todd, art by Anastassia Neislotova

PARENTAL ADVISORY
HELLO KITTY: SURPRISE! is rated A and is suitable for readers of all ages.
RATED A FOR ALL AGES
ratings.viz.com

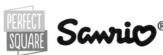

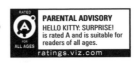

Contents

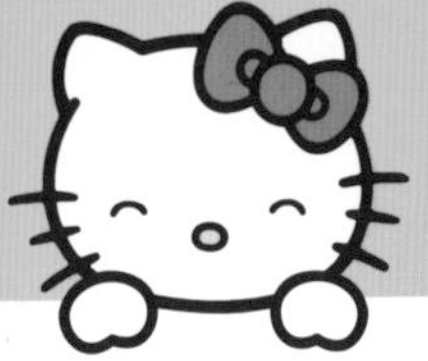

Family

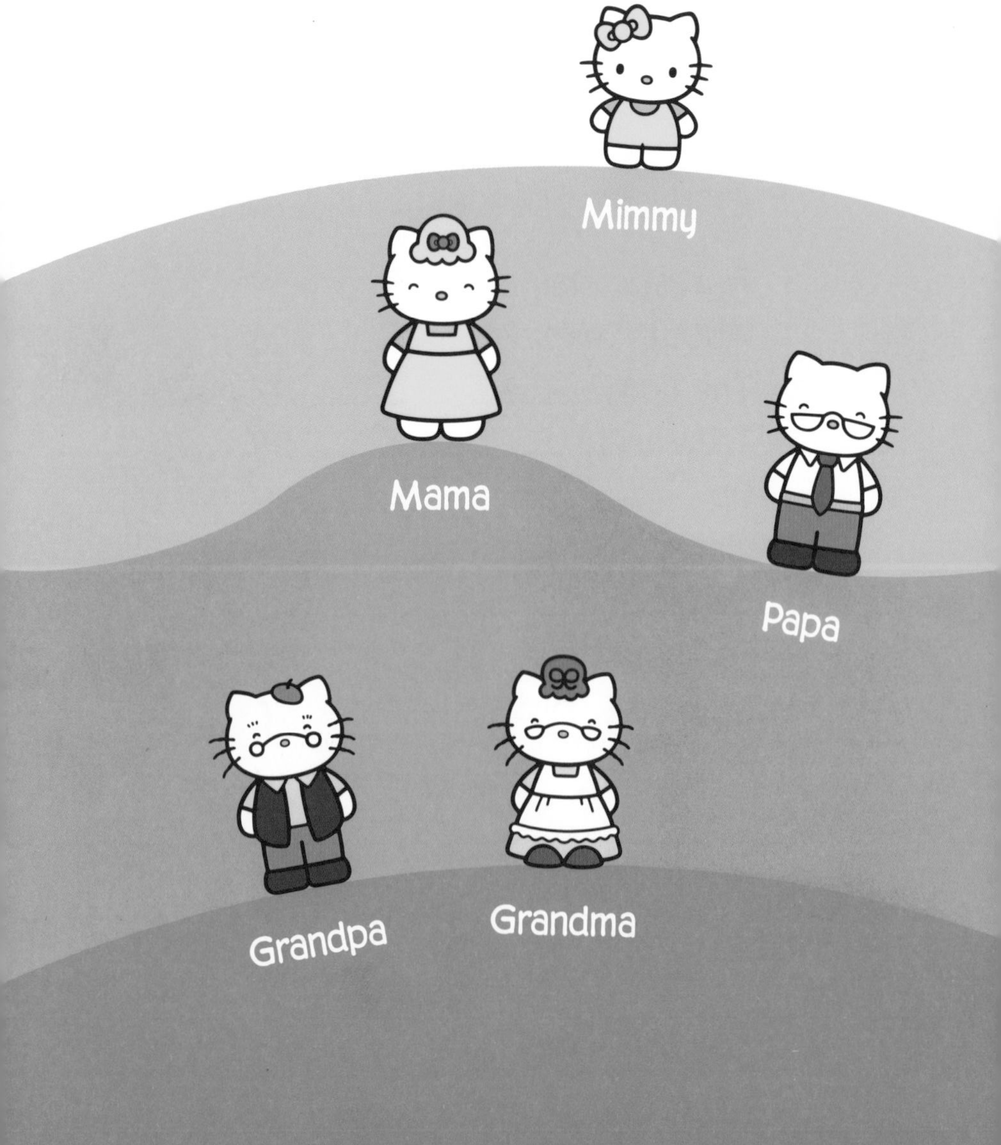
Mimmy
Mama
Papa
Grandpa
Grandma

and Friends

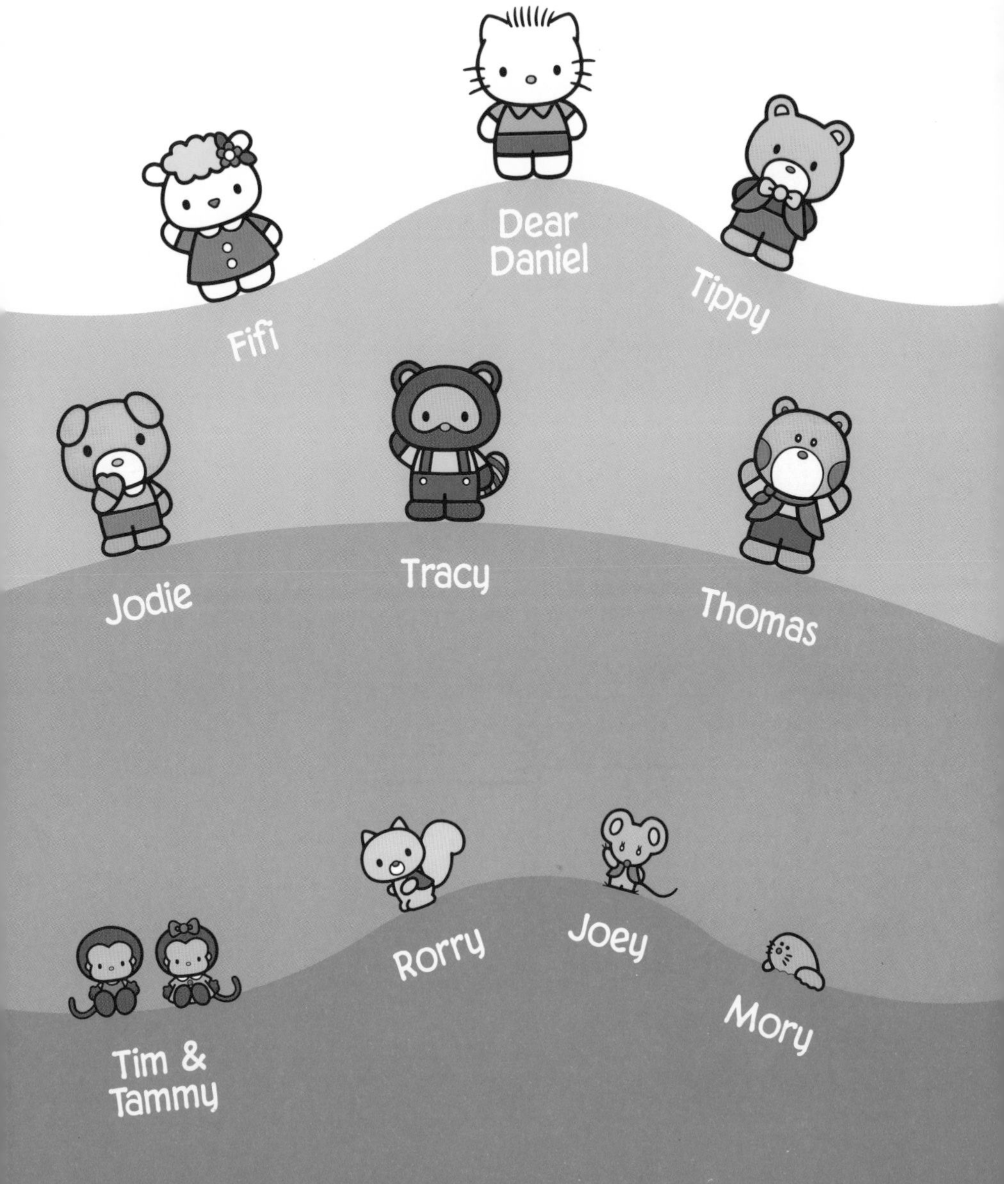
Dear Daniel
Fifi
Tippy
Jodie
Tracy
Thomas
Rorry
Joey
Tim & Tammy
Mory

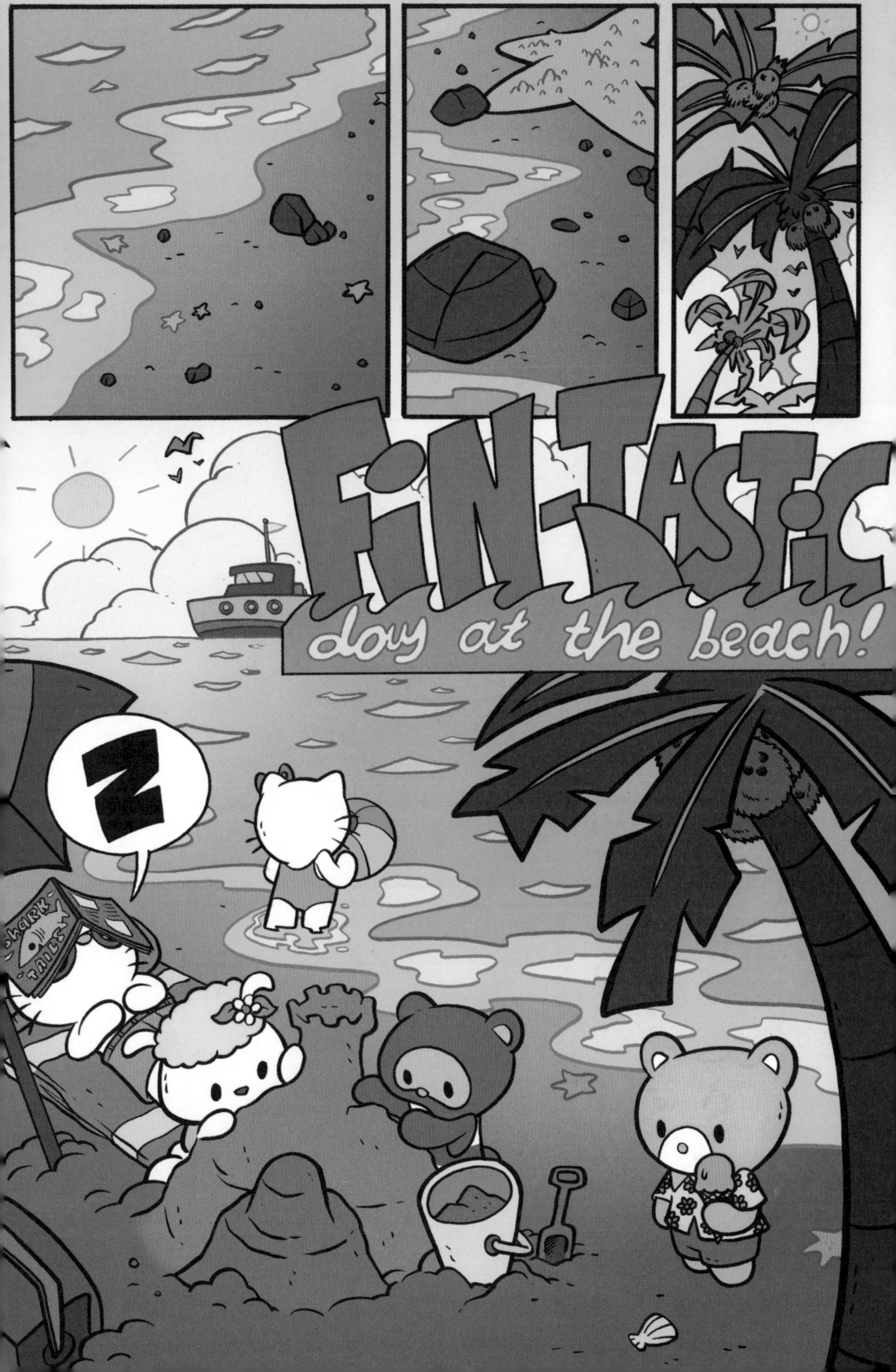
FIN-TASTIC
day at the beach!
Z
SHARK TAILS

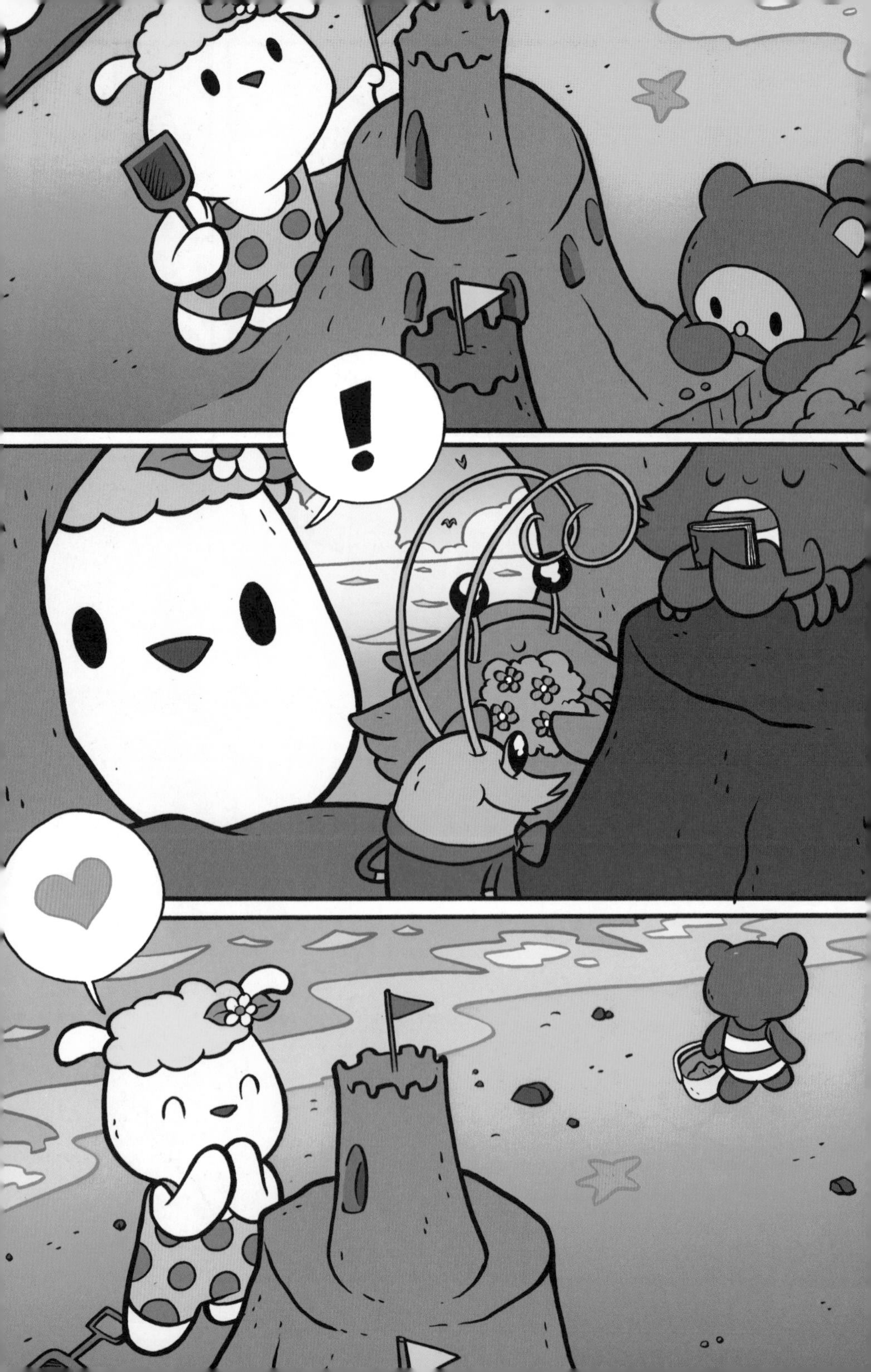
!

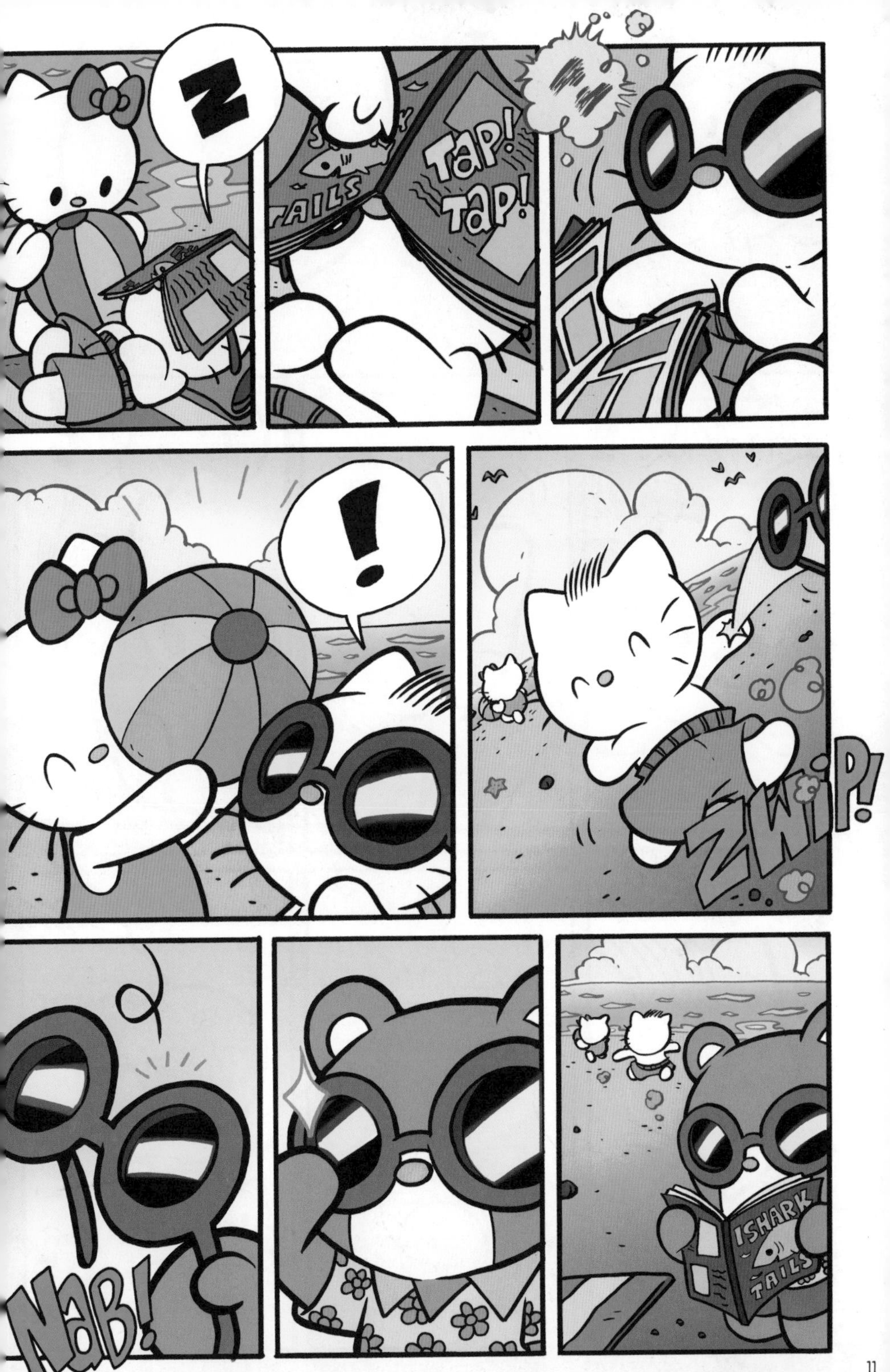
Z
SHARK TAILS
TAP! TAP!
!
ZWIP!
NAB!
SHARK TAILS

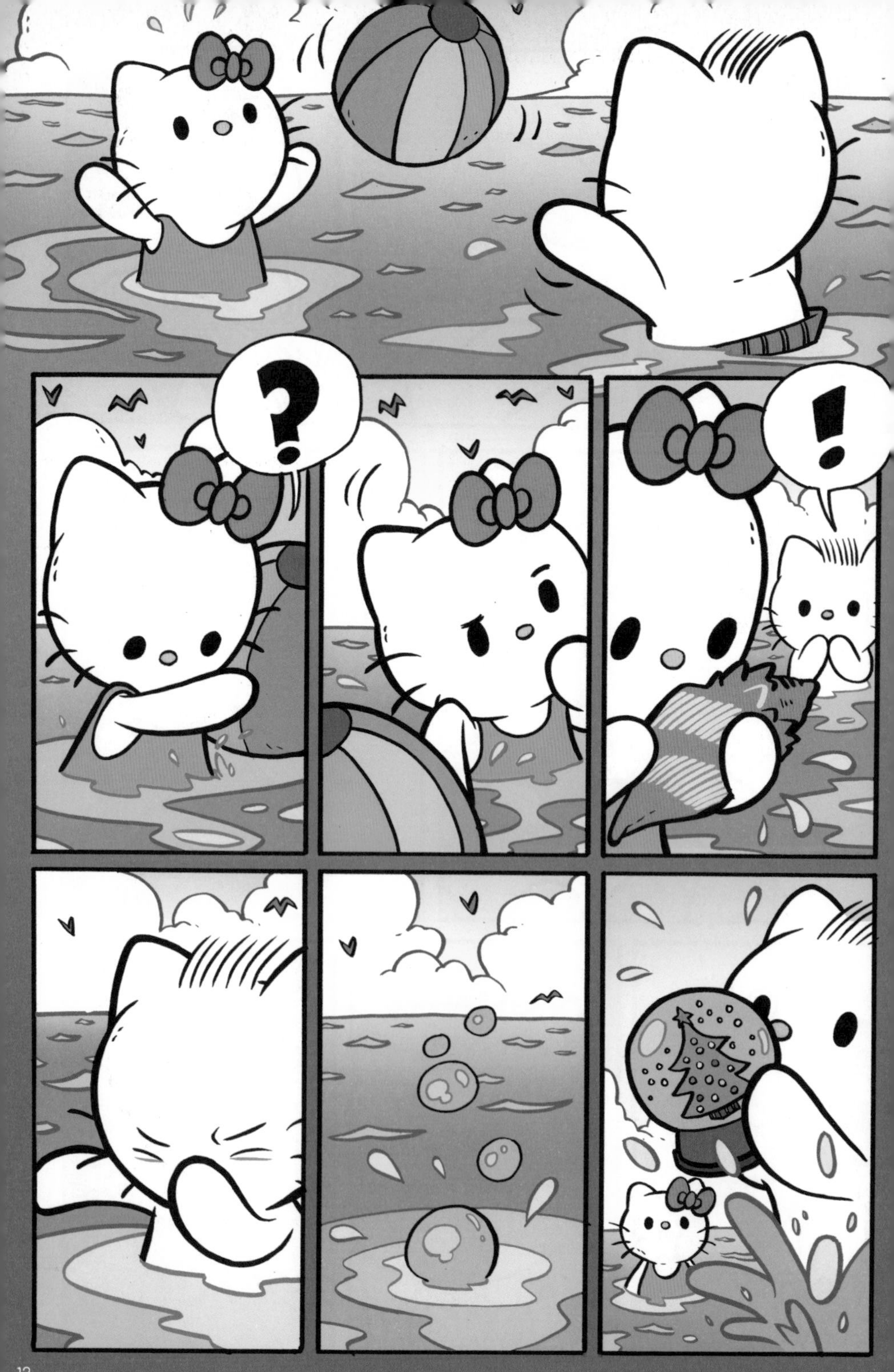
?
!

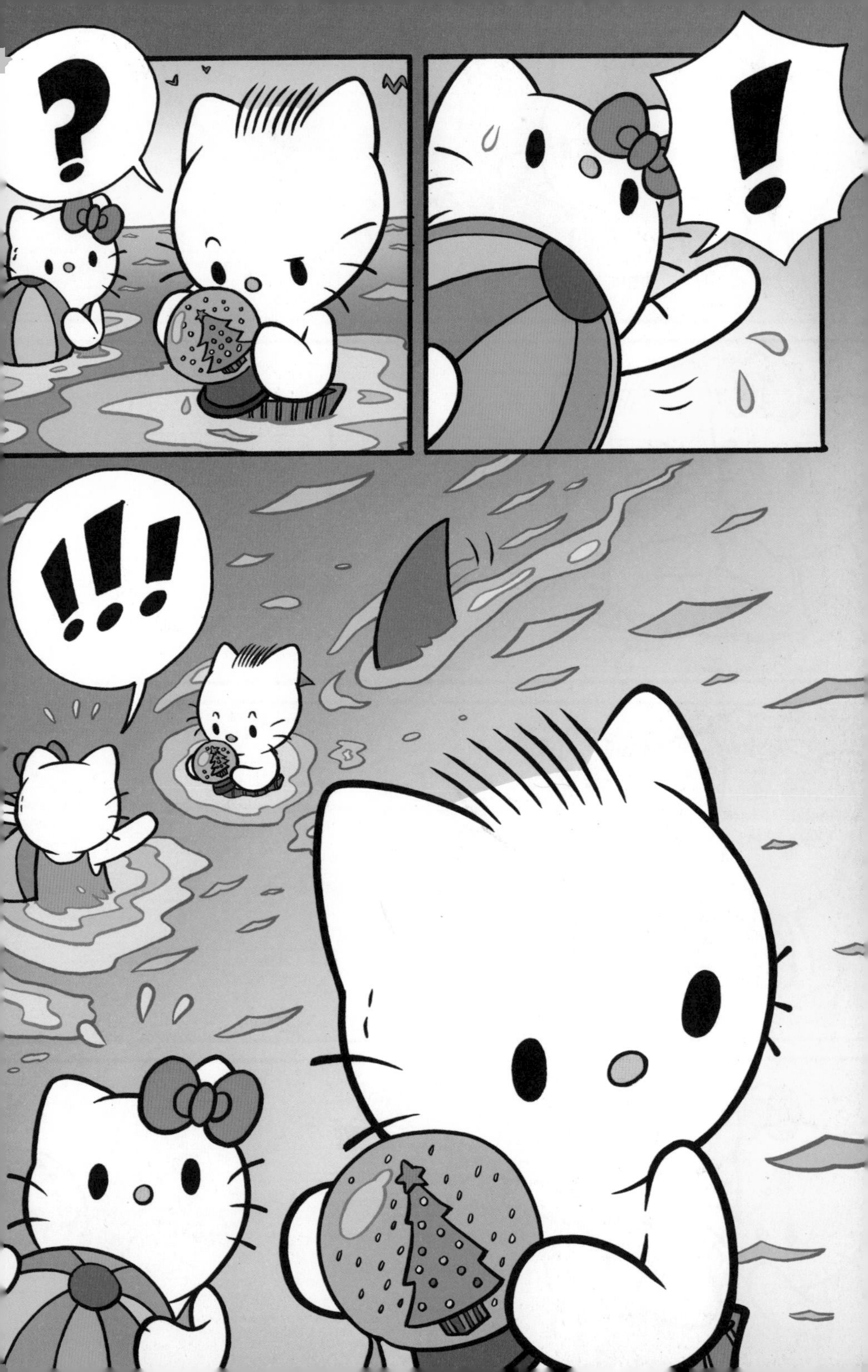
?
!
!!!

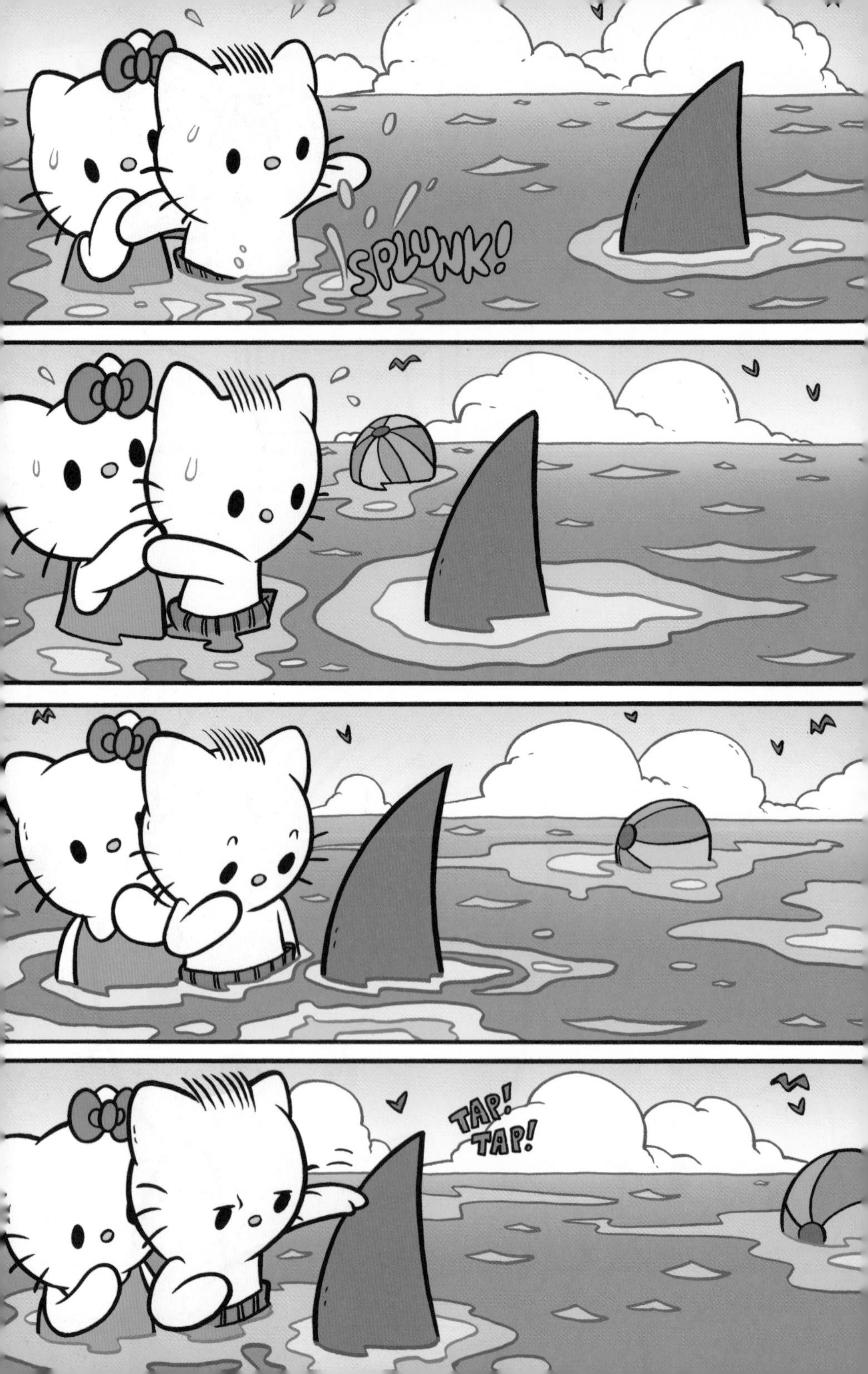
SPLUNK!
TAP!
TAP!

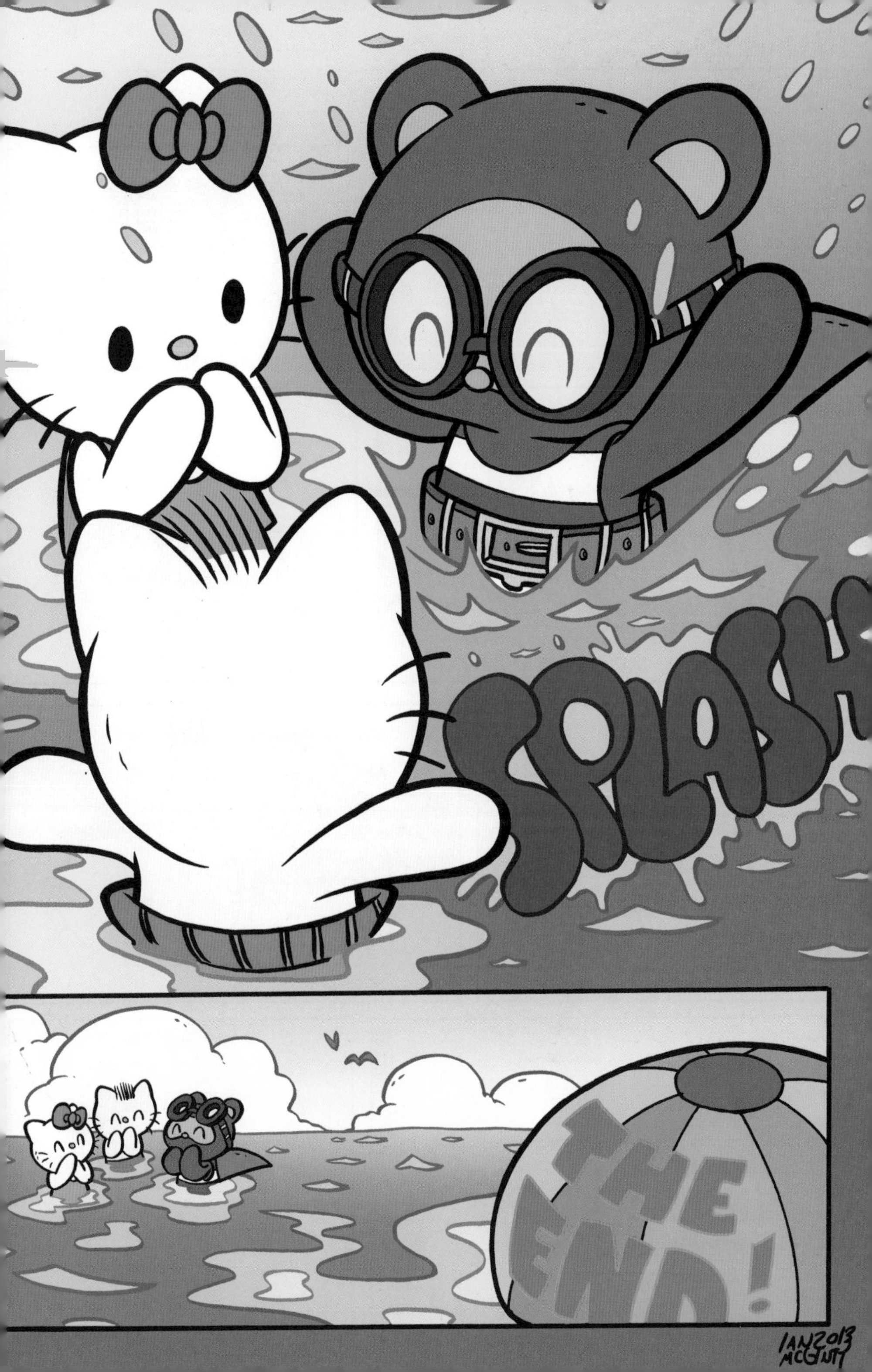

SPLASH
THE END!
IAN 2013 MCGINTY

ABOUT TIME.

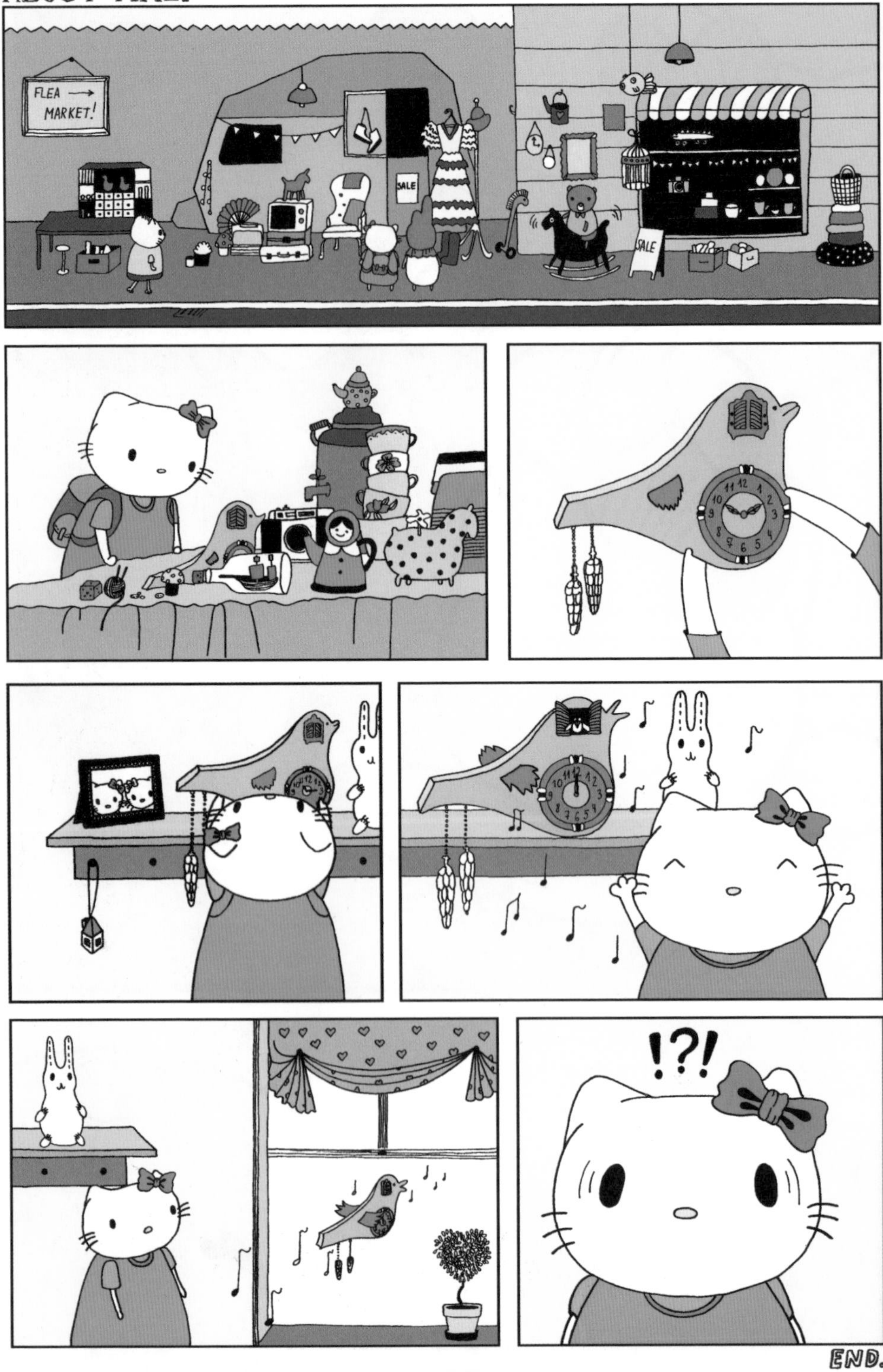
FLEA → MARKET!
SALE
SALE
!?!

END.

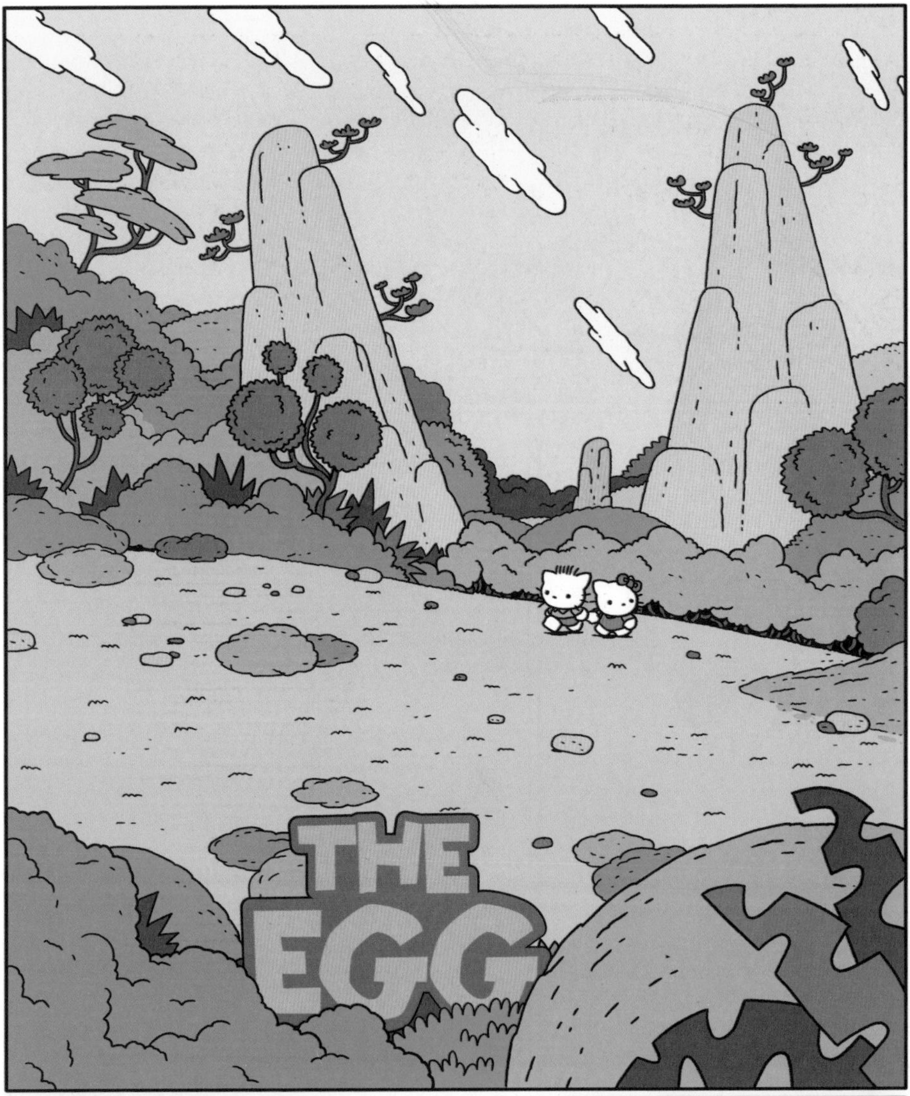
THE EGG

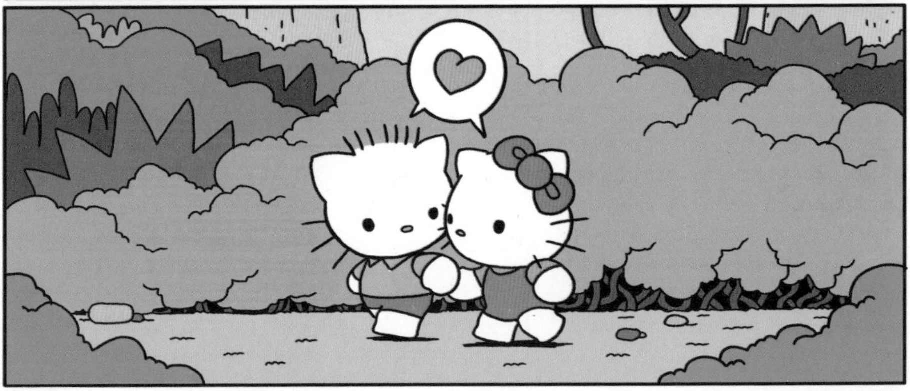

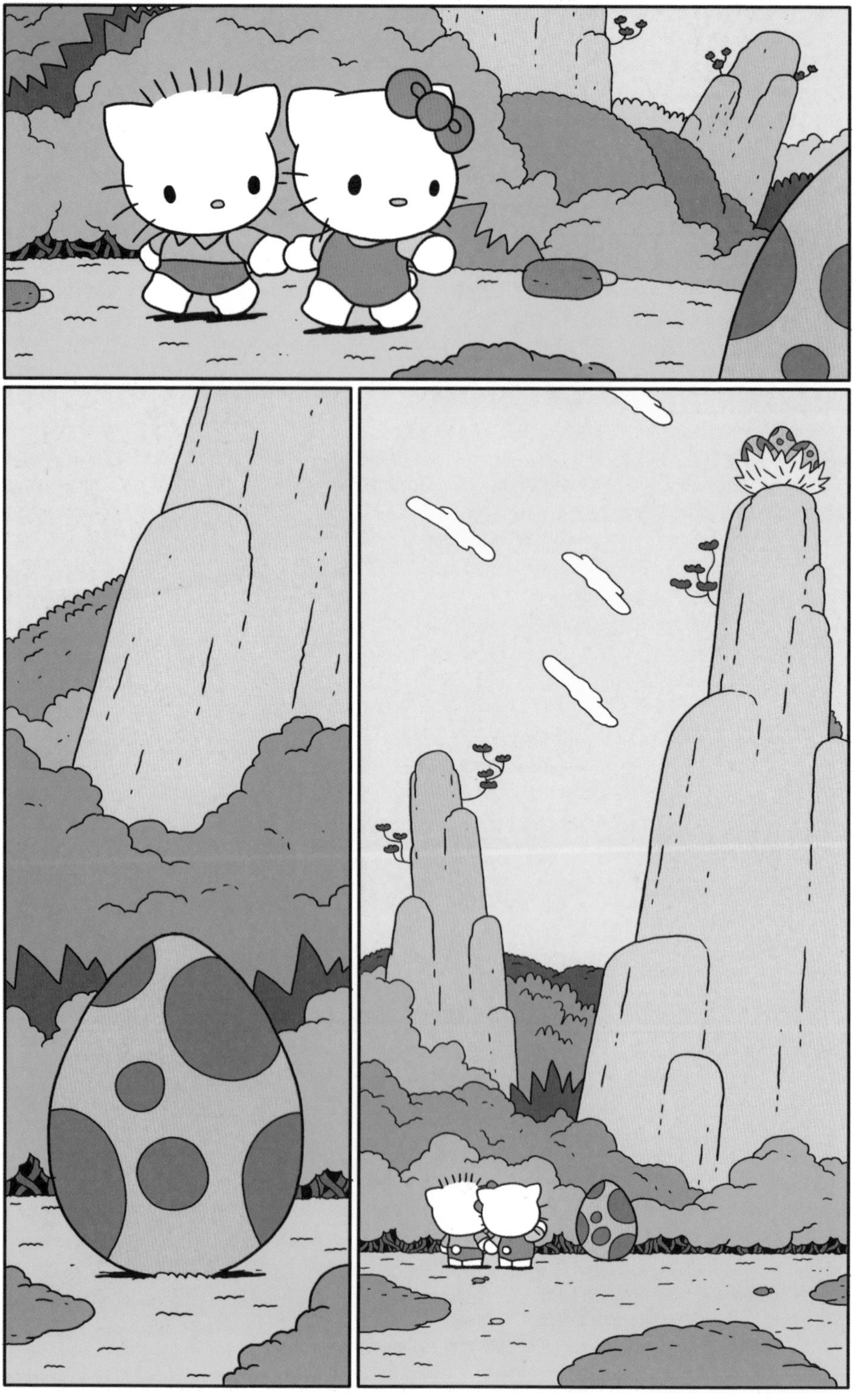

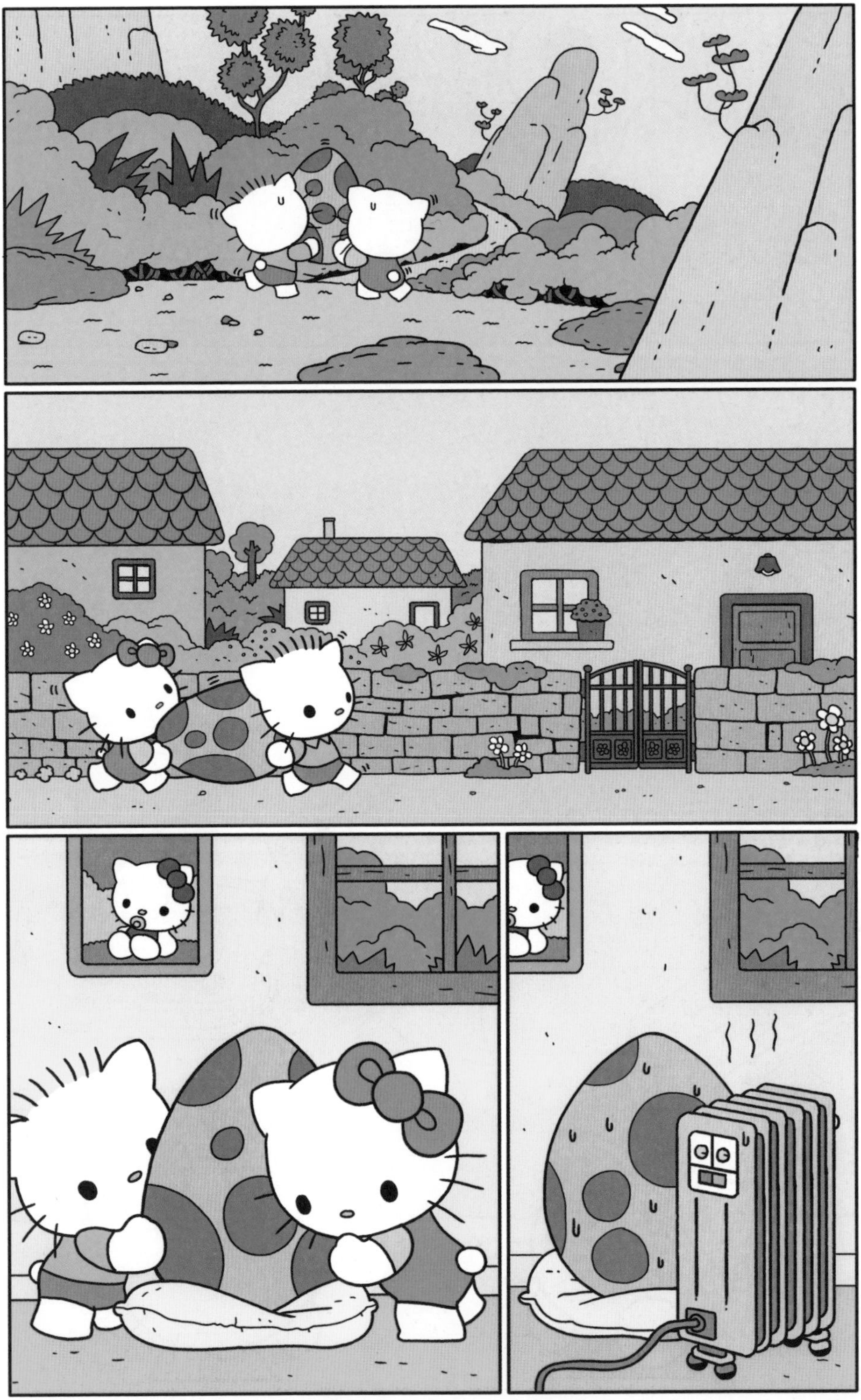

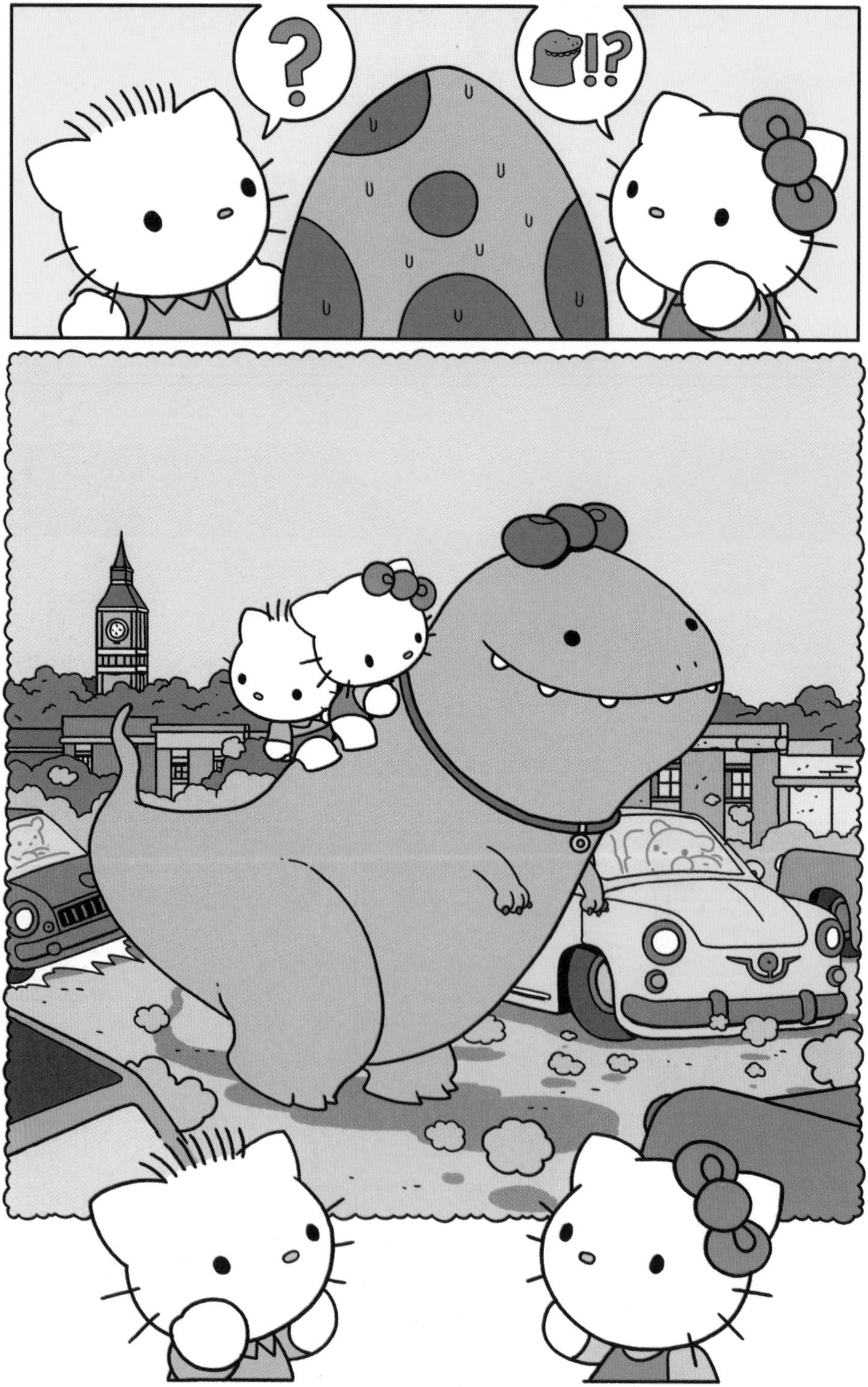
?
!?

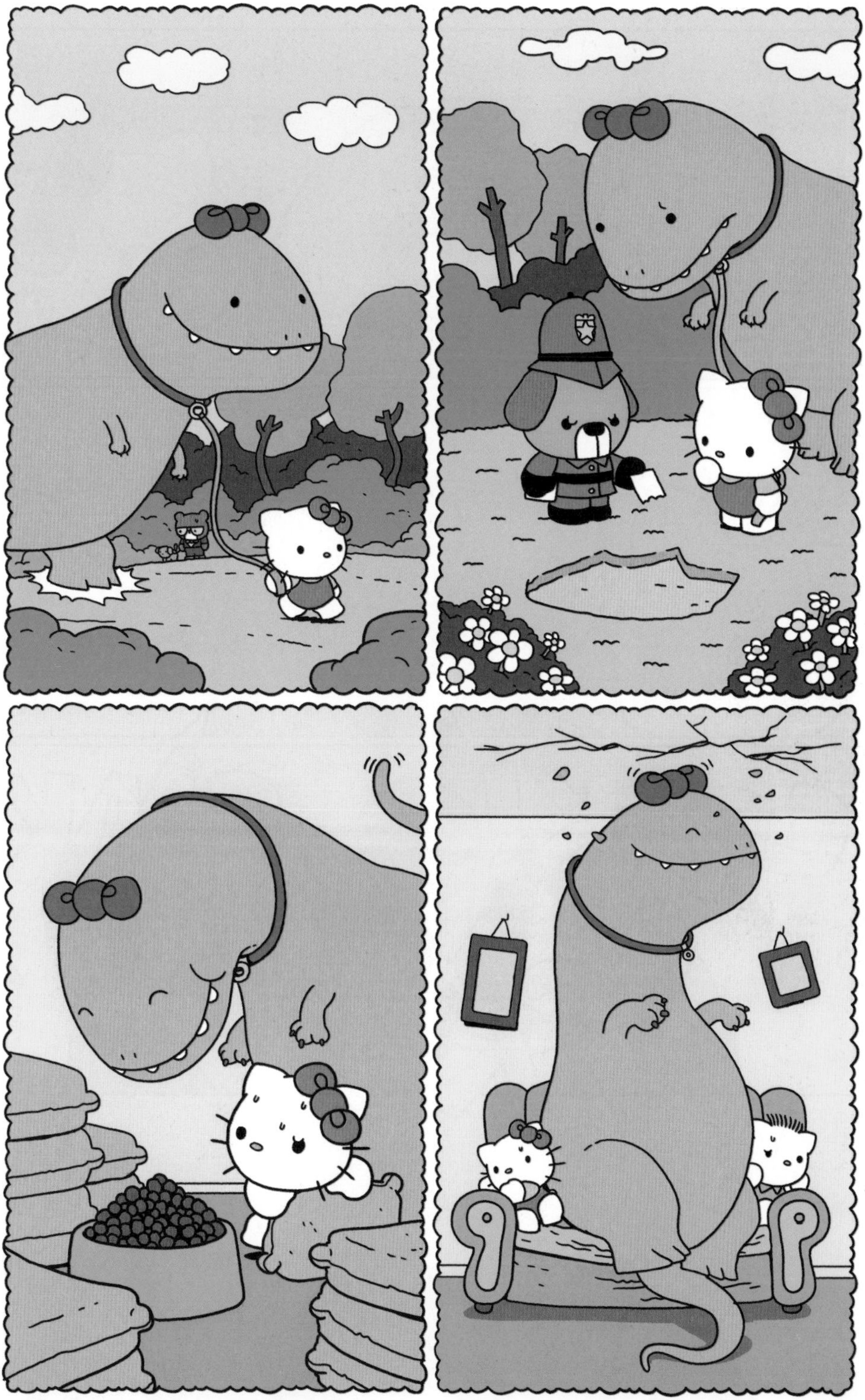

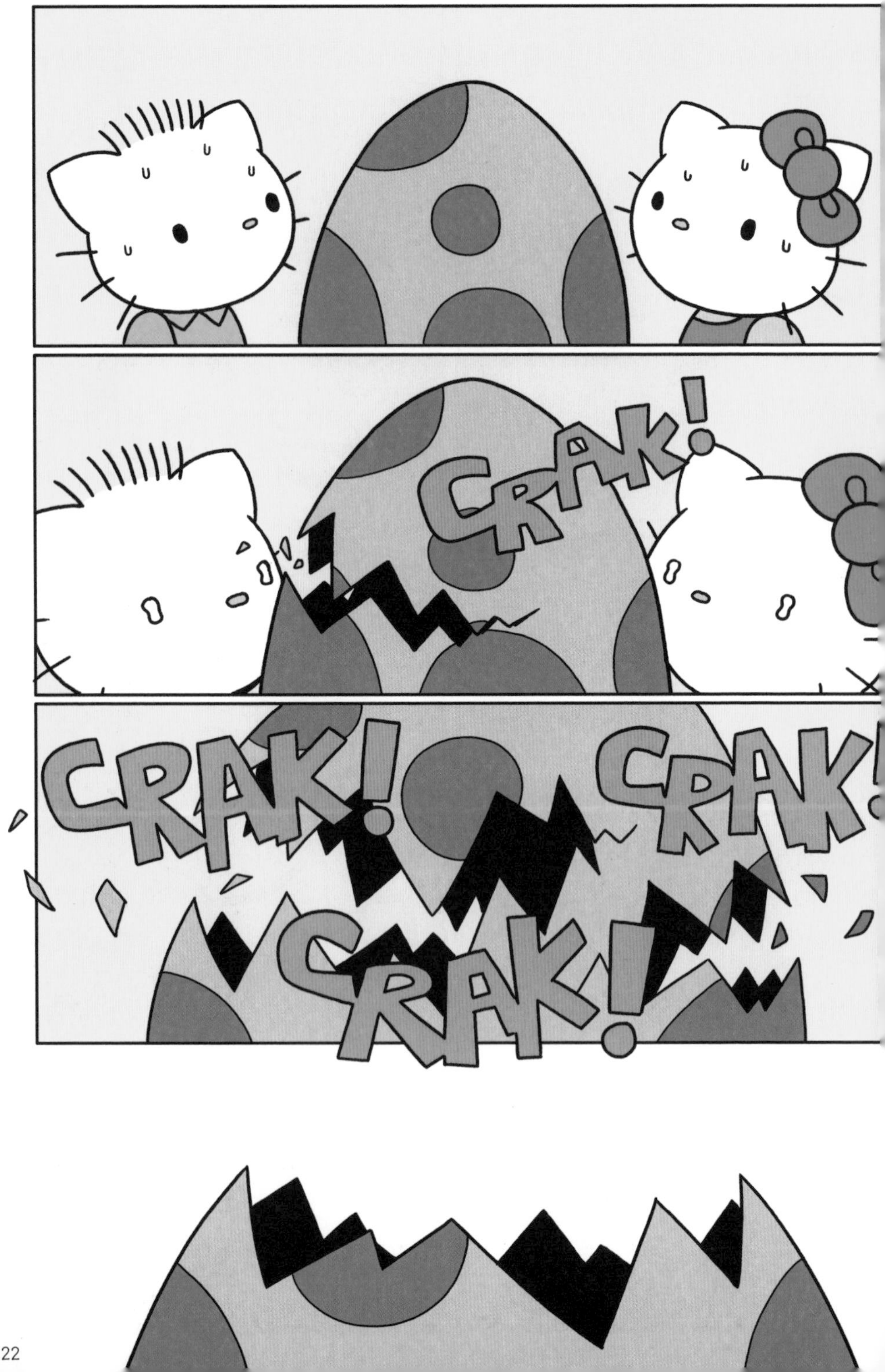
CRAK!
CRAK!
CRAK!
CRAK!

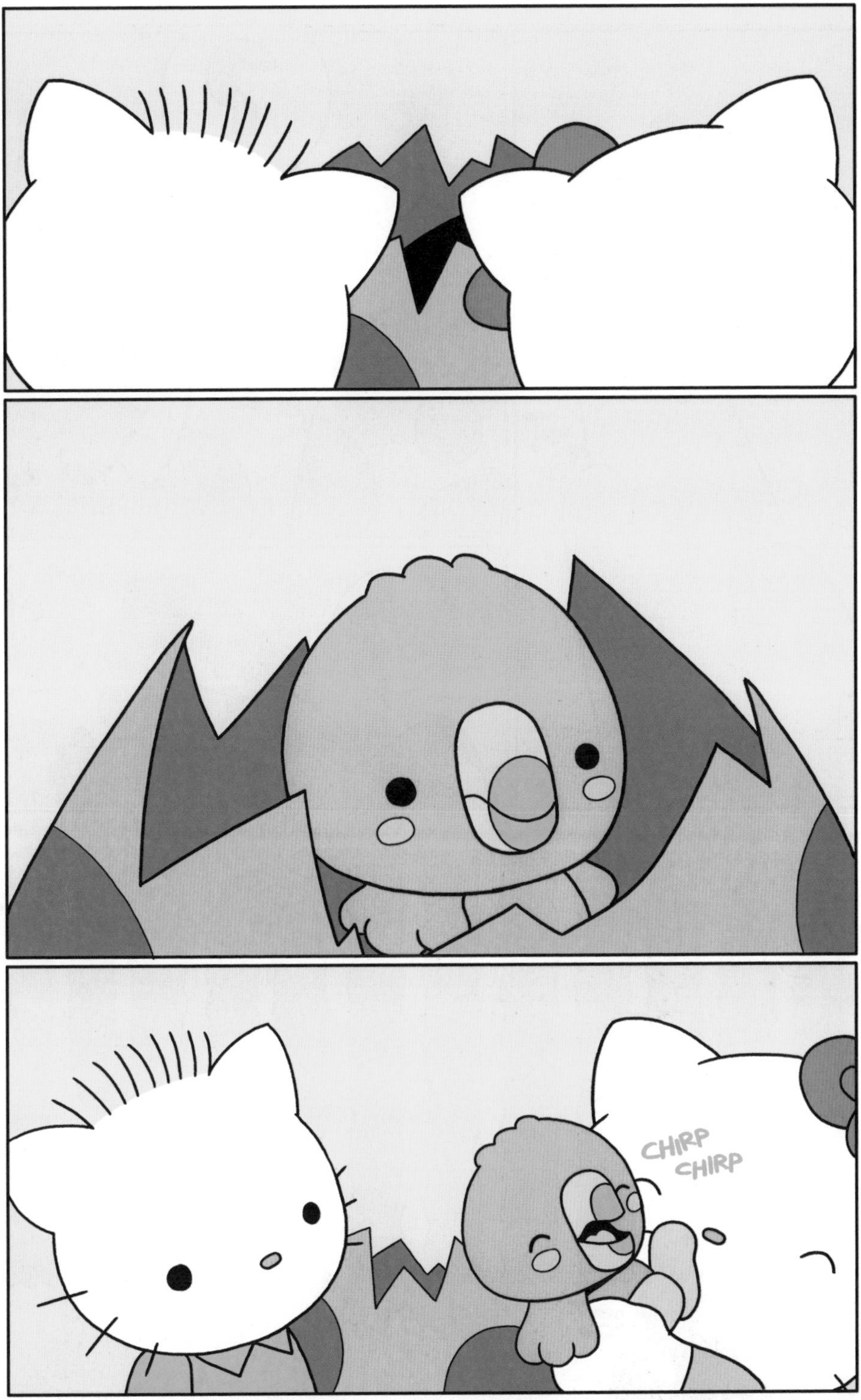
CHIRP
CHIRP

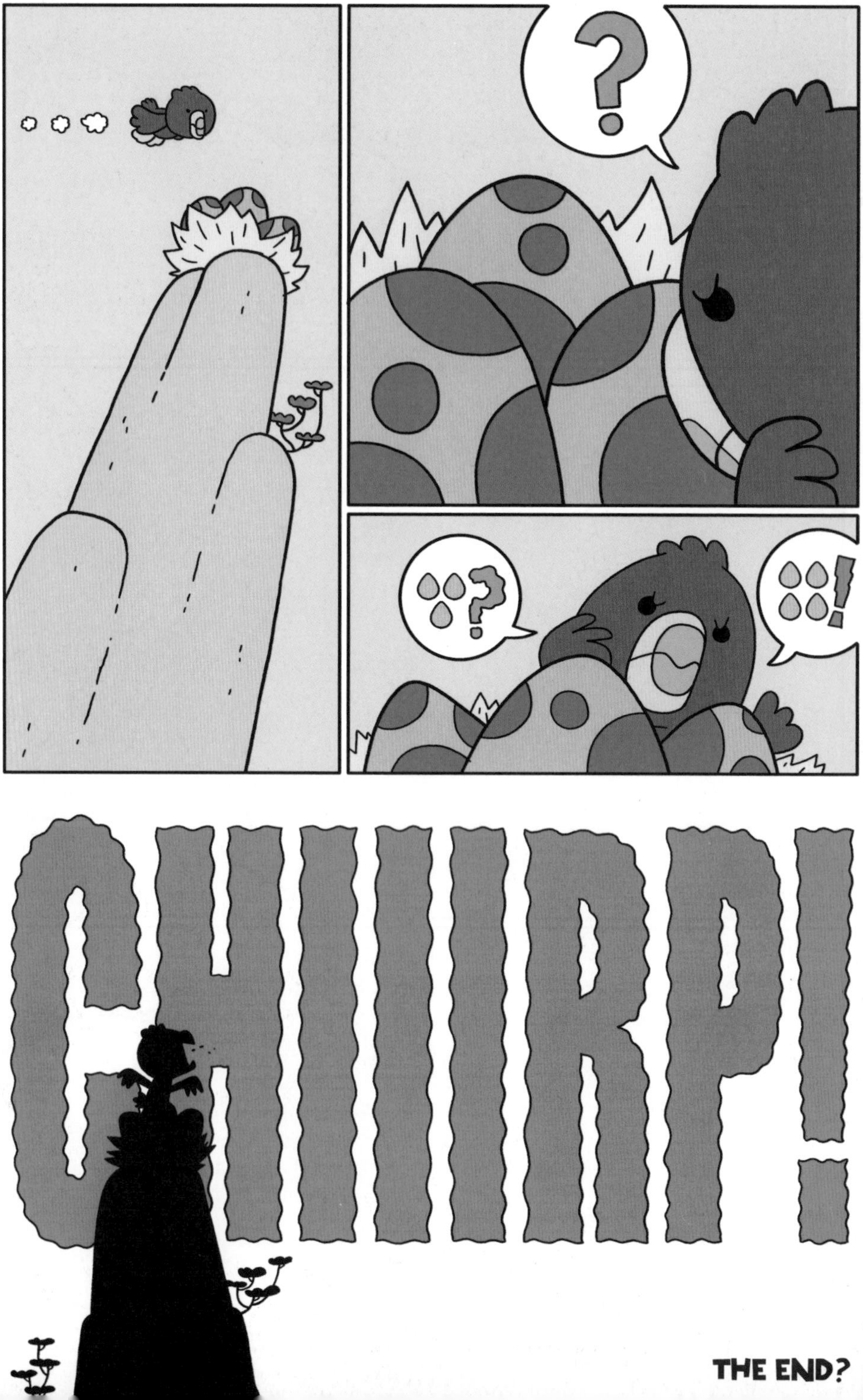
?
??
!
CHIRP!
THE END?

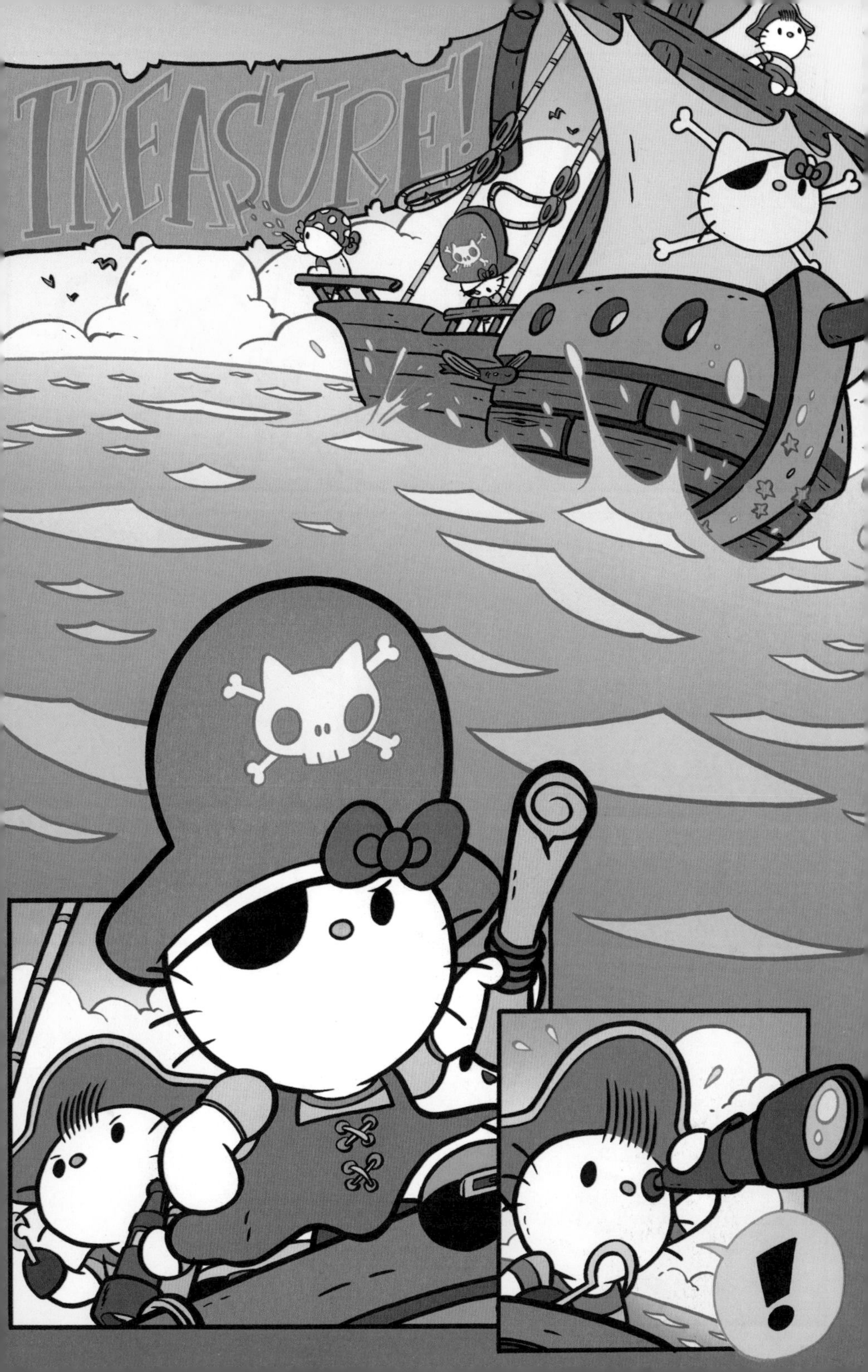
TREASURE!
!

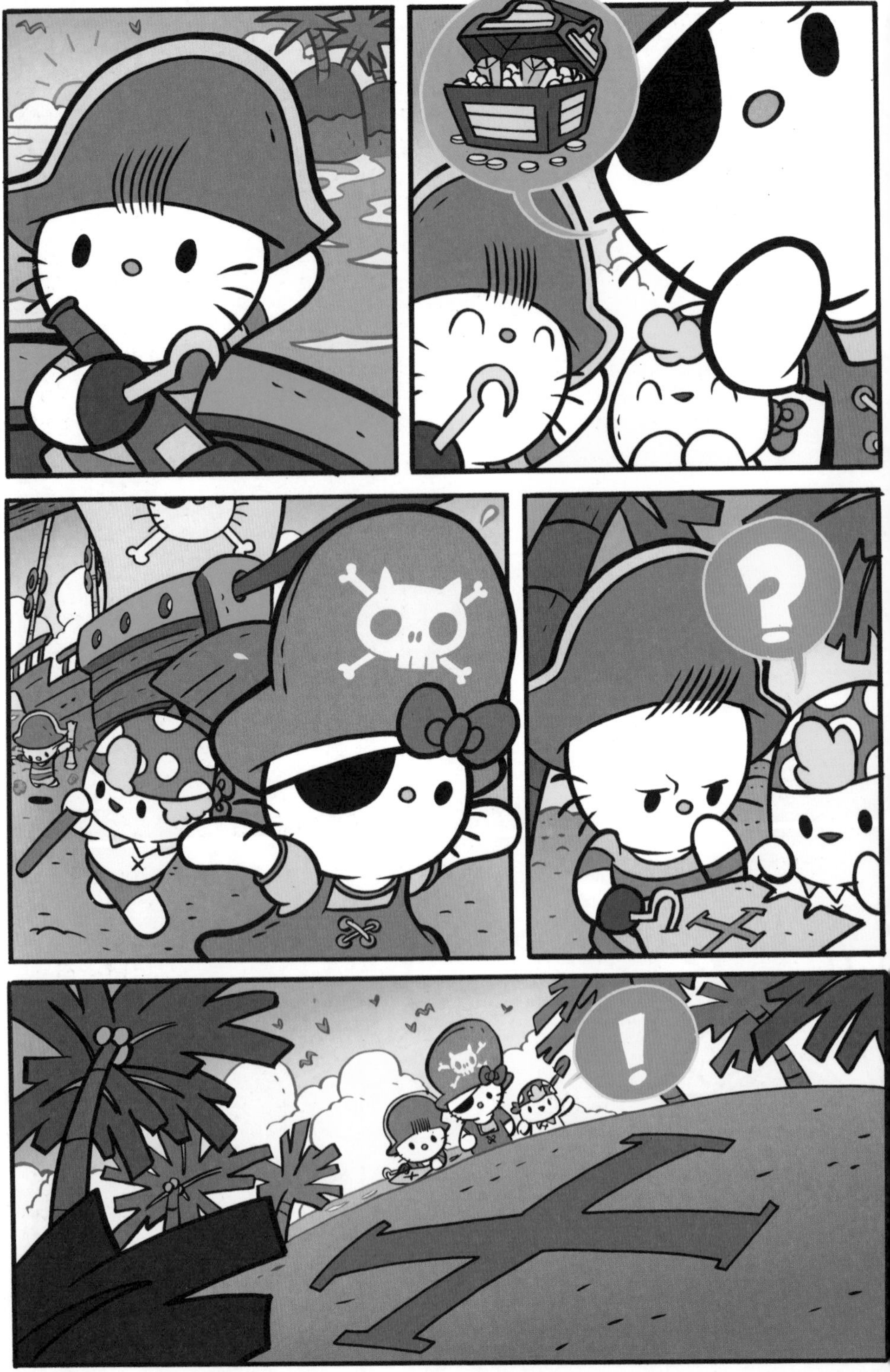
?
!

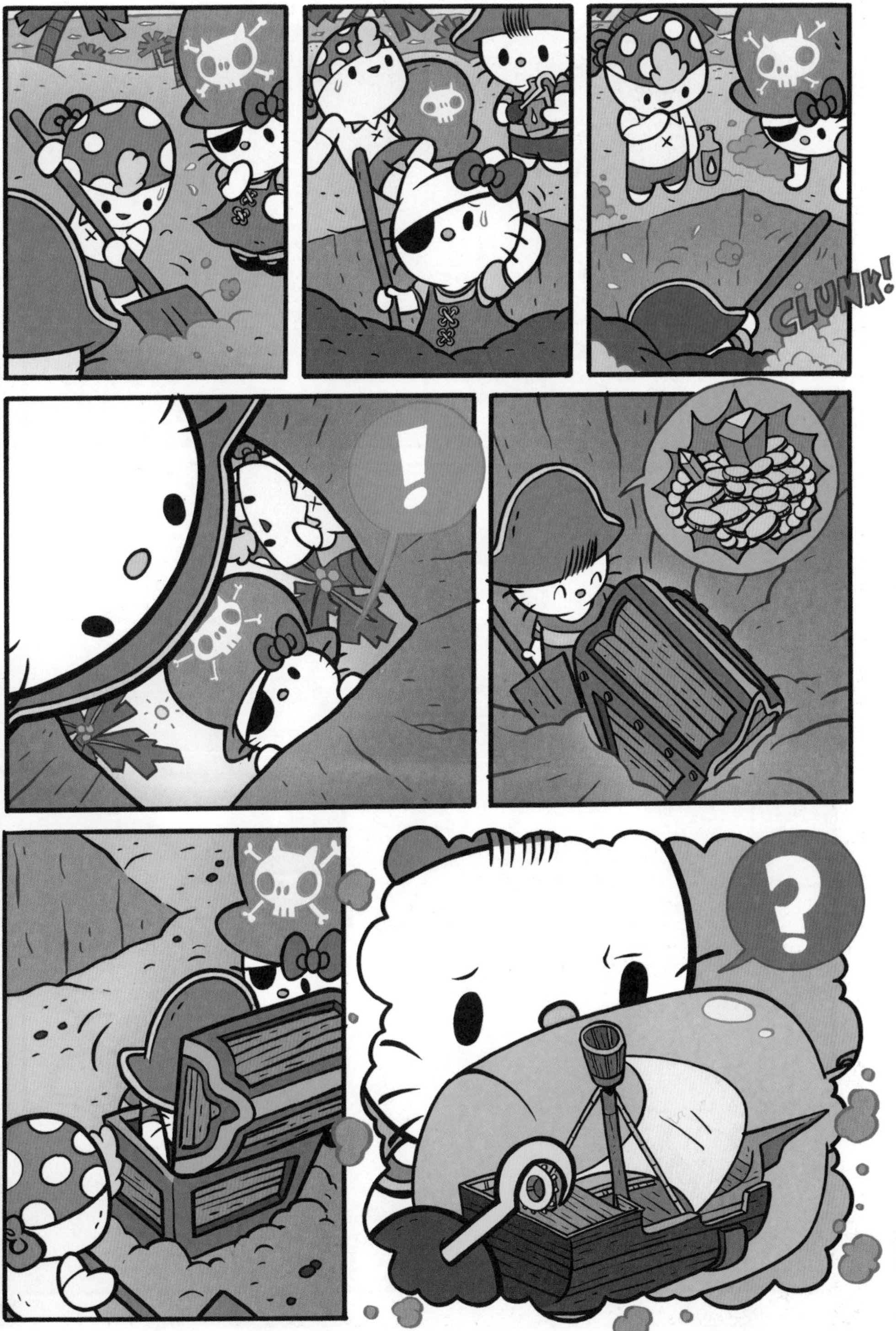
CLUNK!
!
?

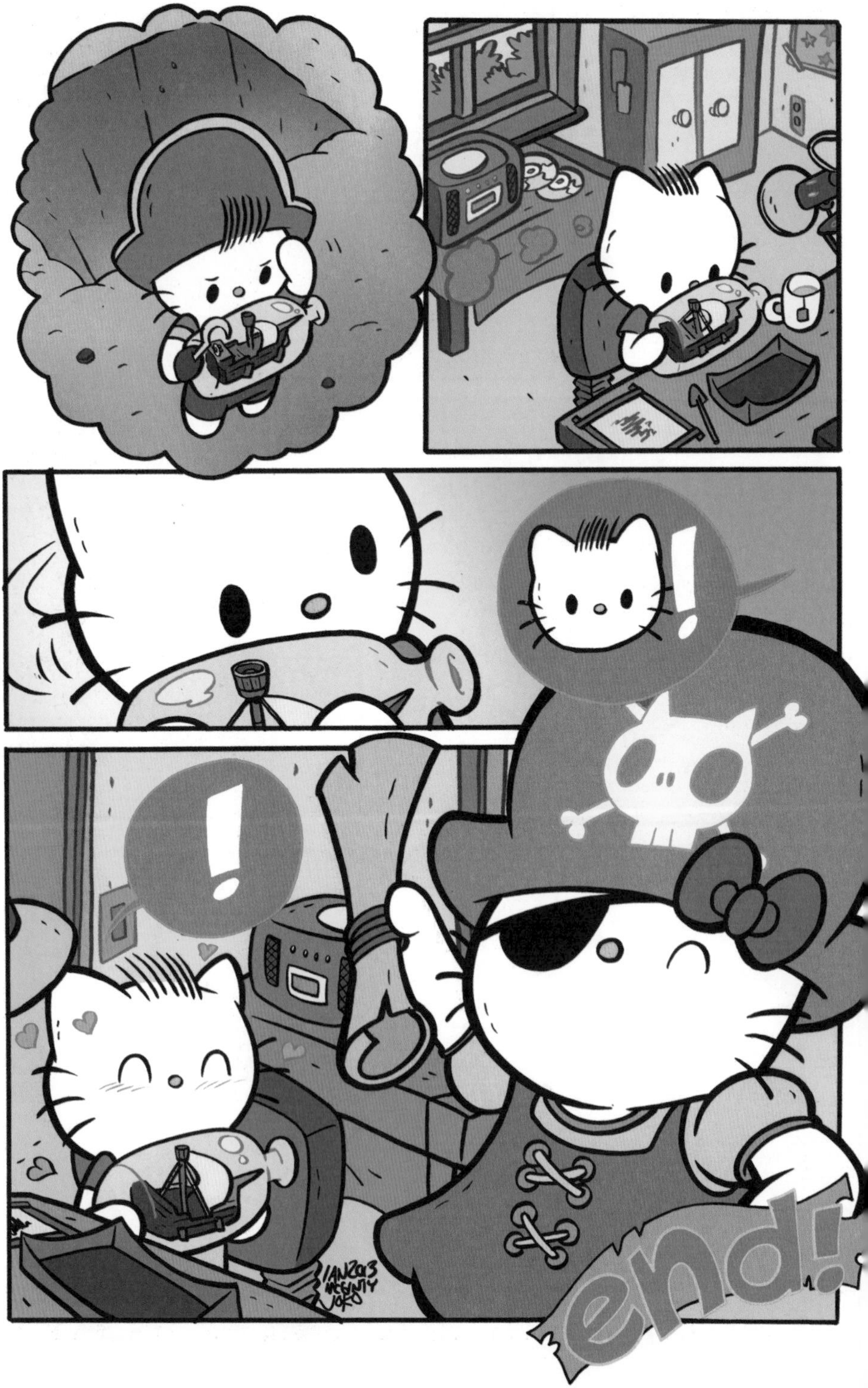
!
!
end!

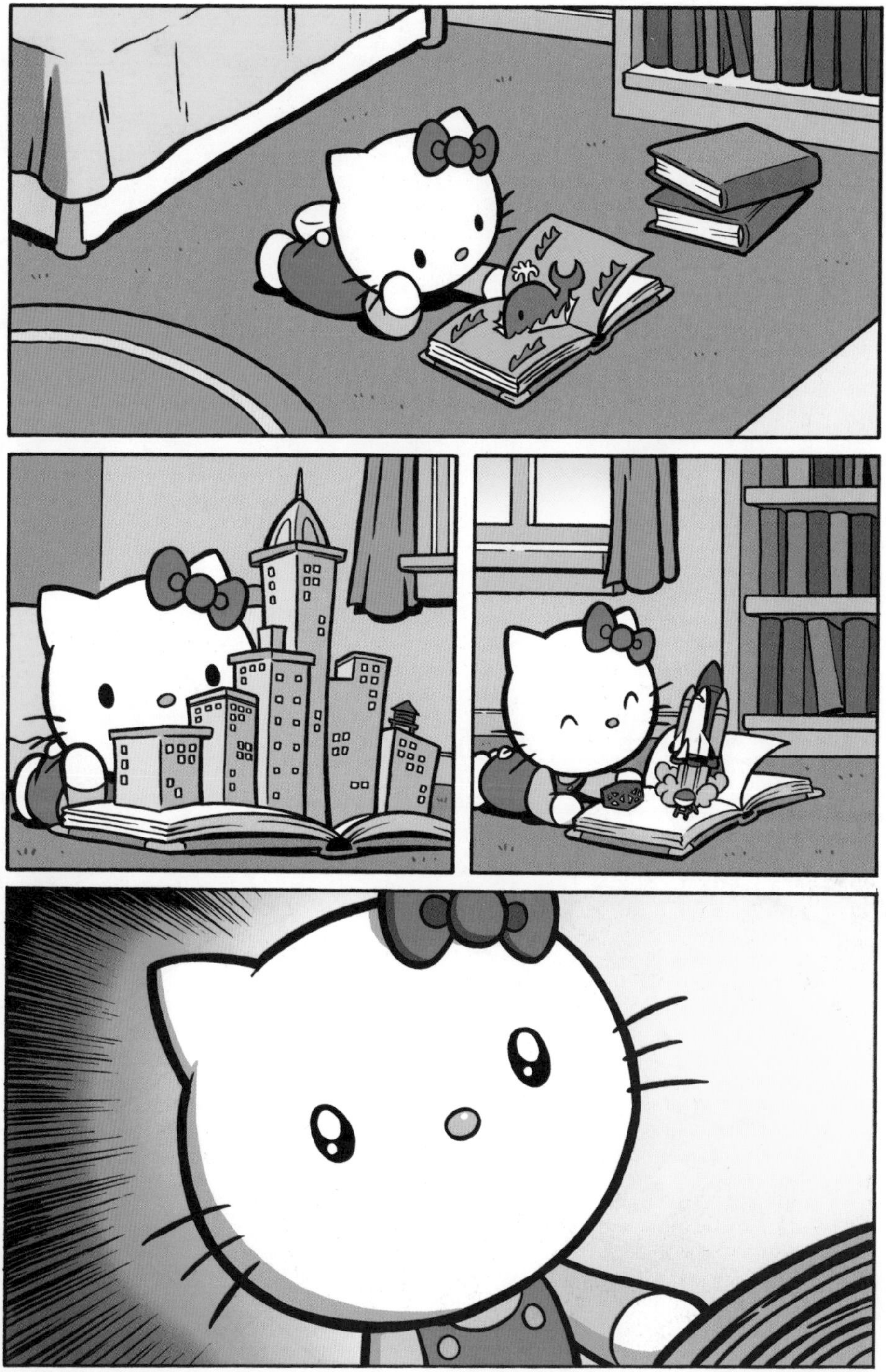

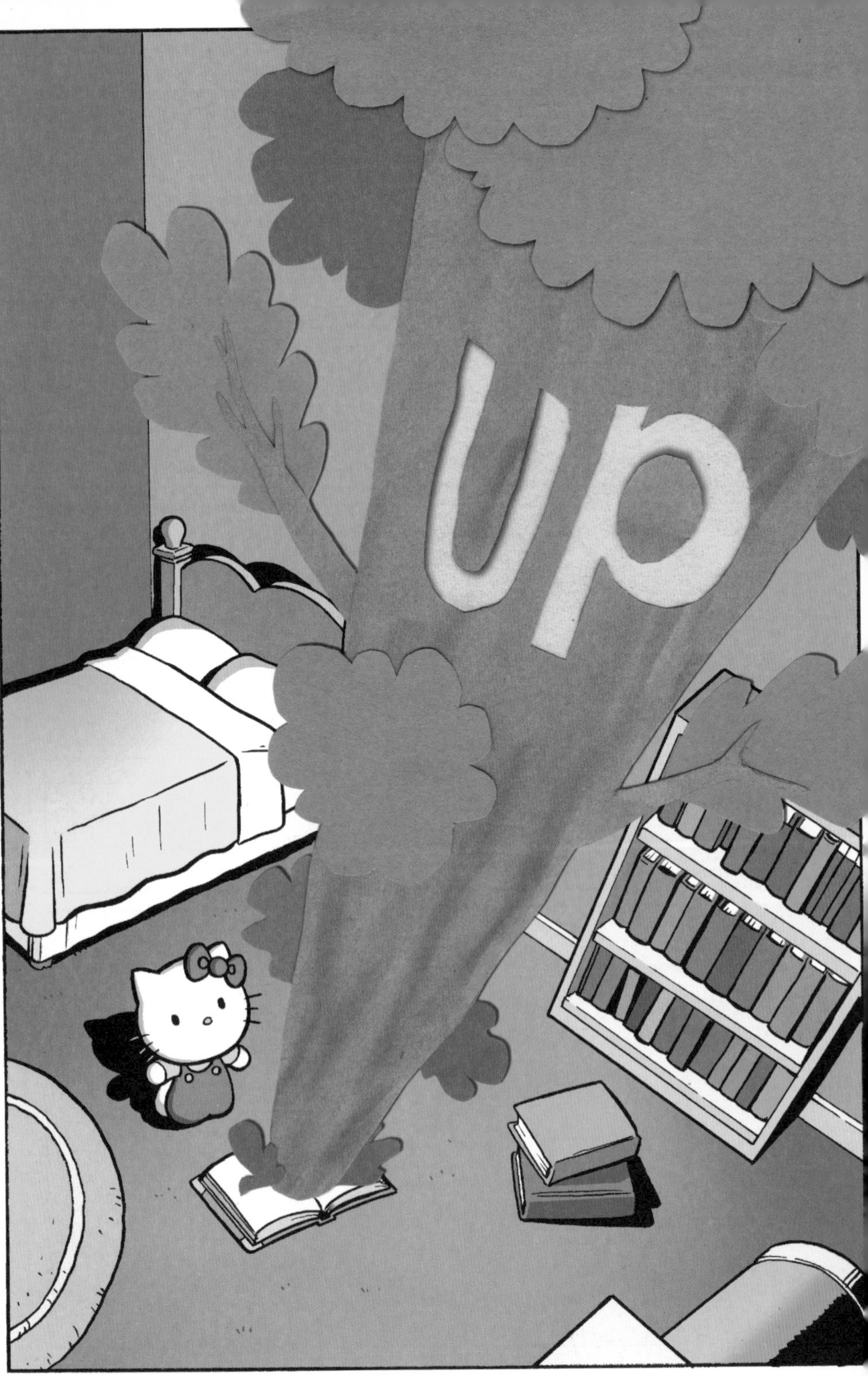
up

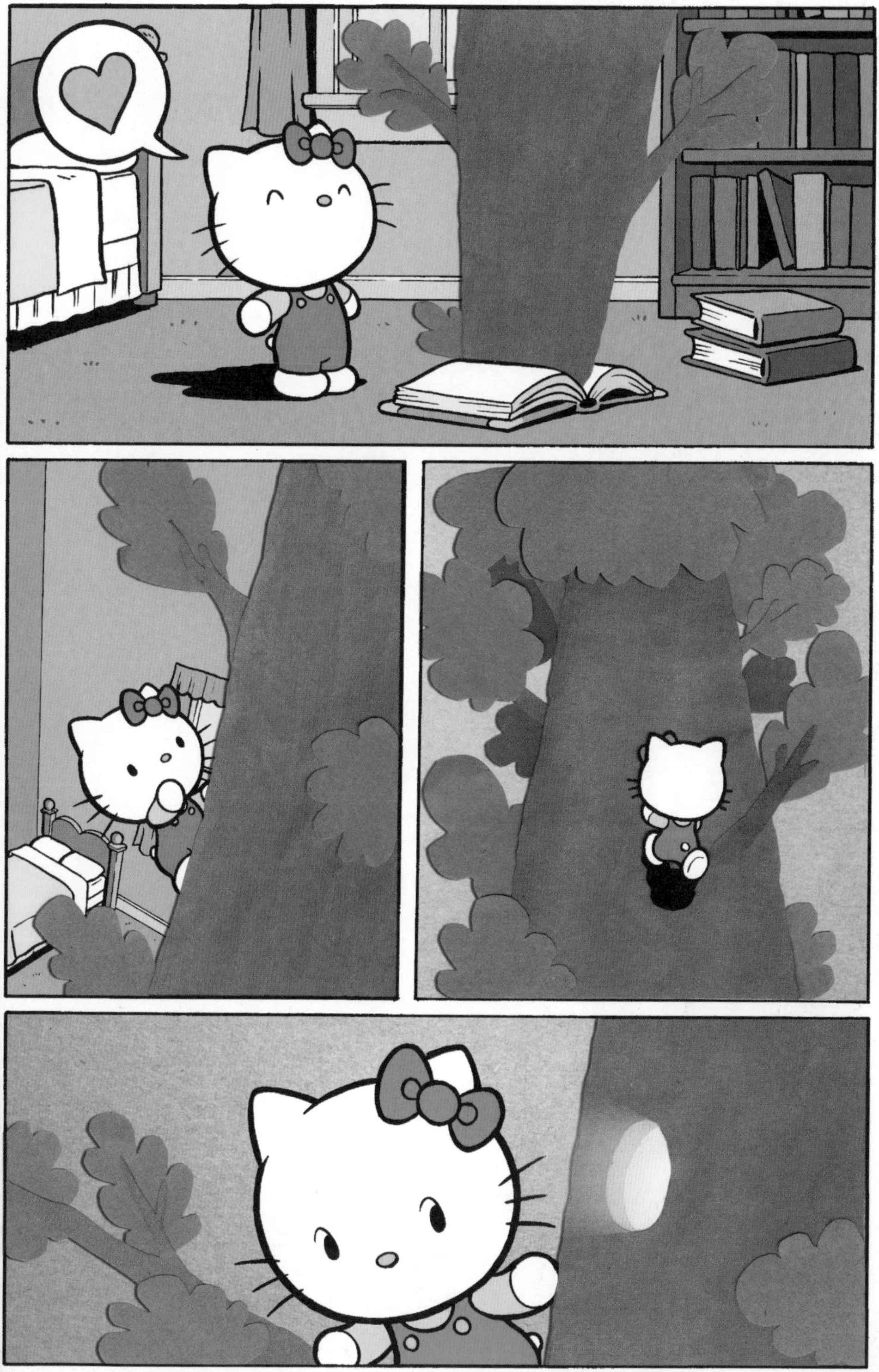

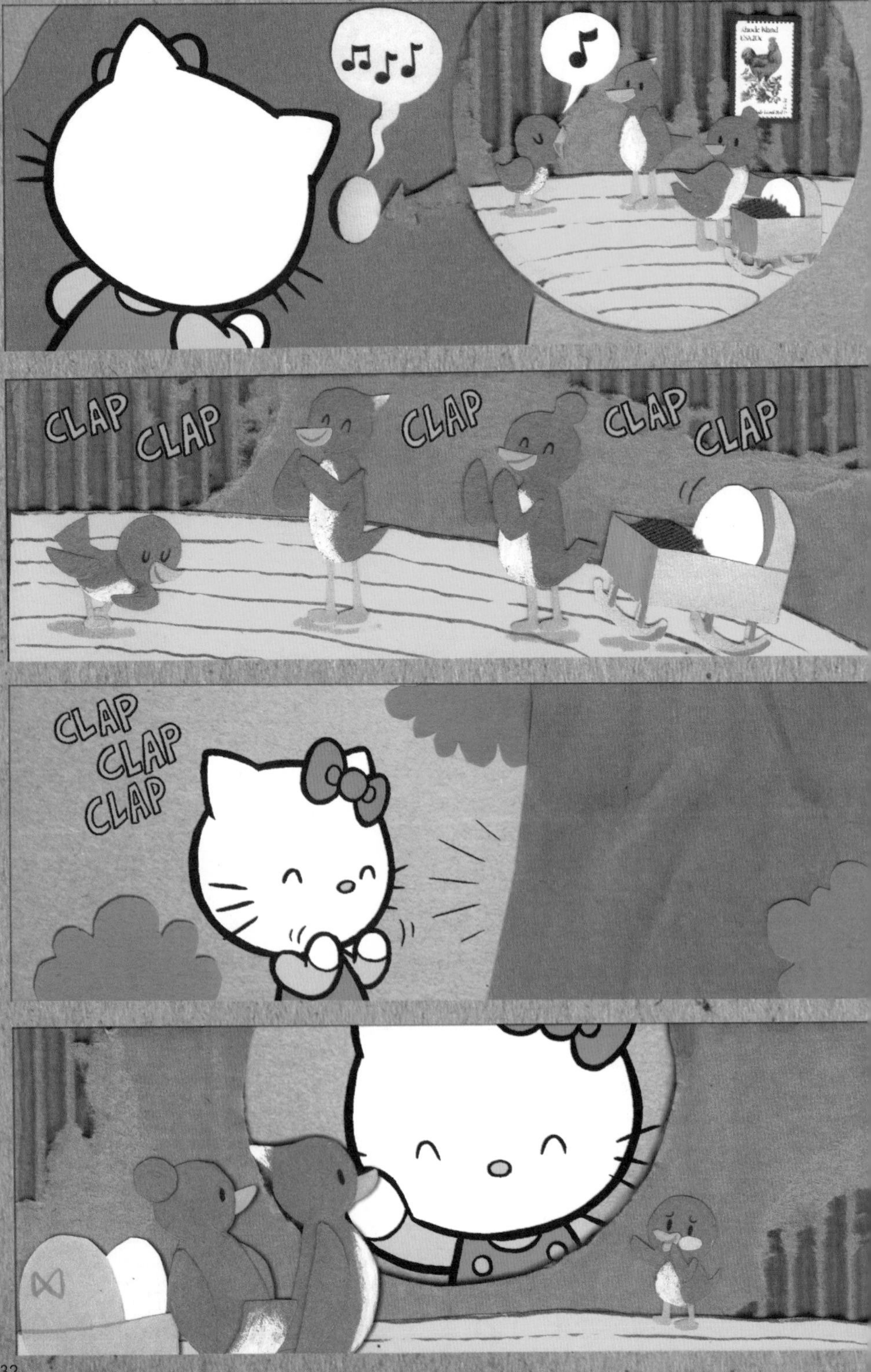
CLAP
CLAP
CLAP
CLAP
CLAP
CLAP
CLAP
CLAP

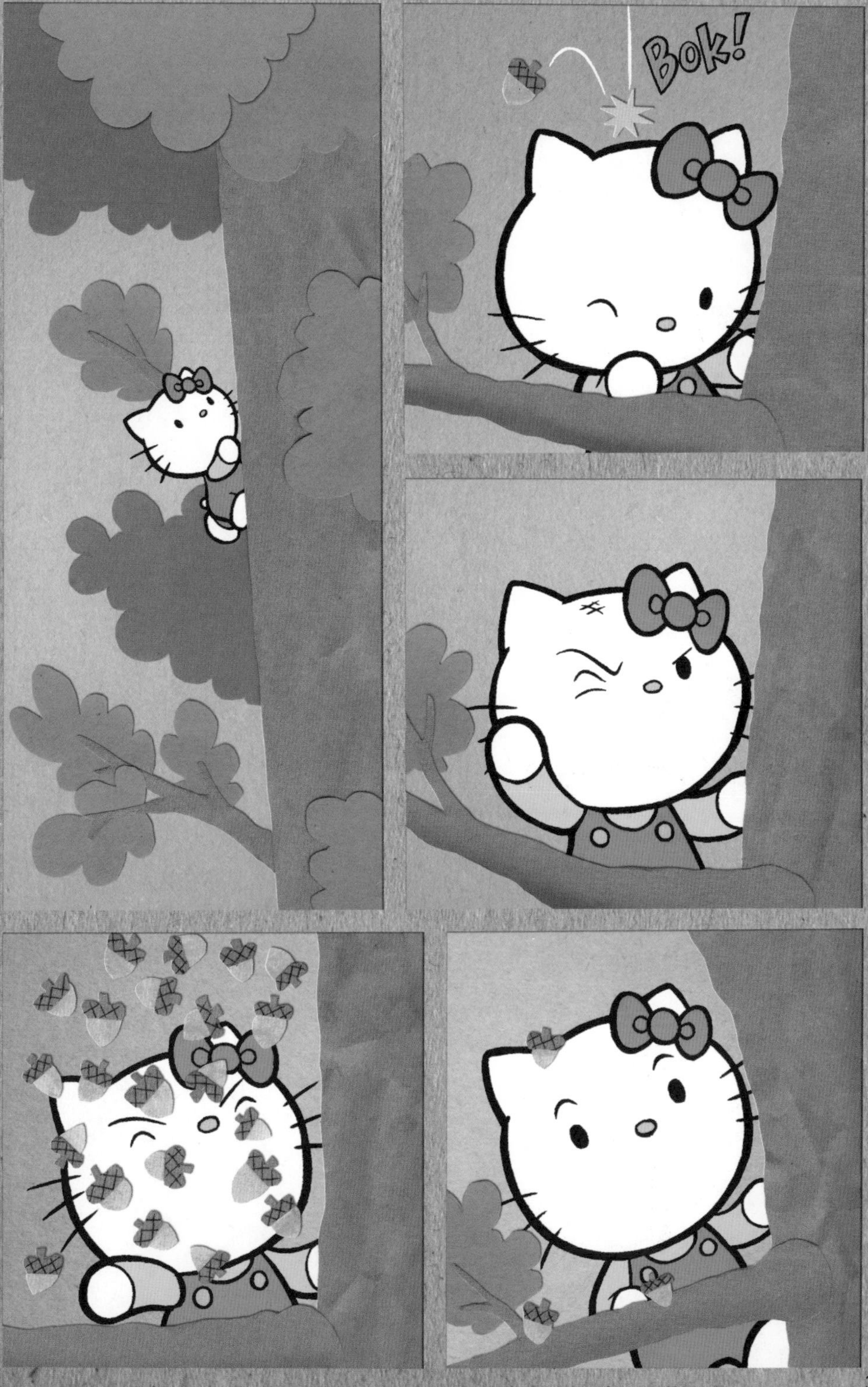
Bok!

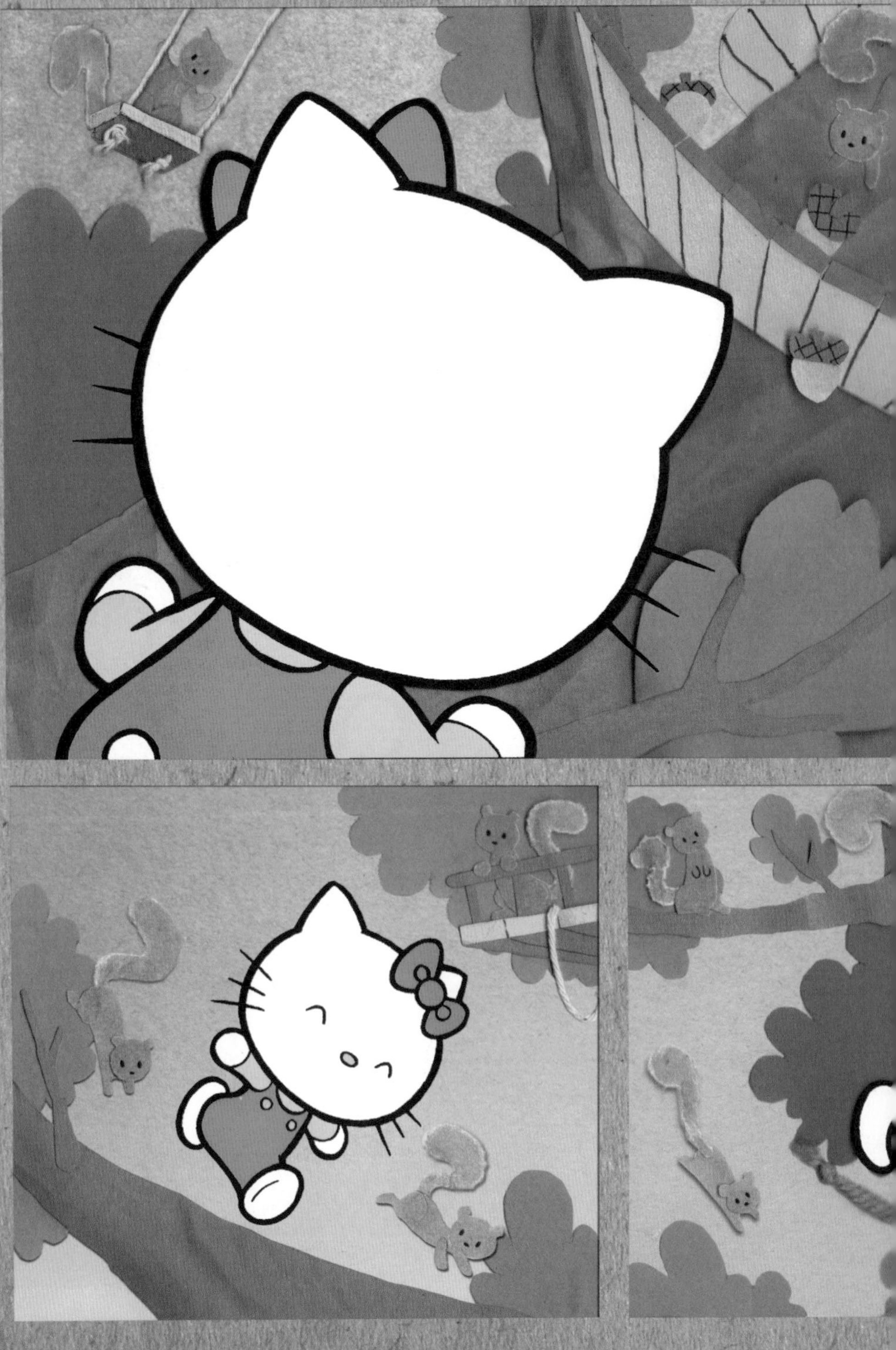

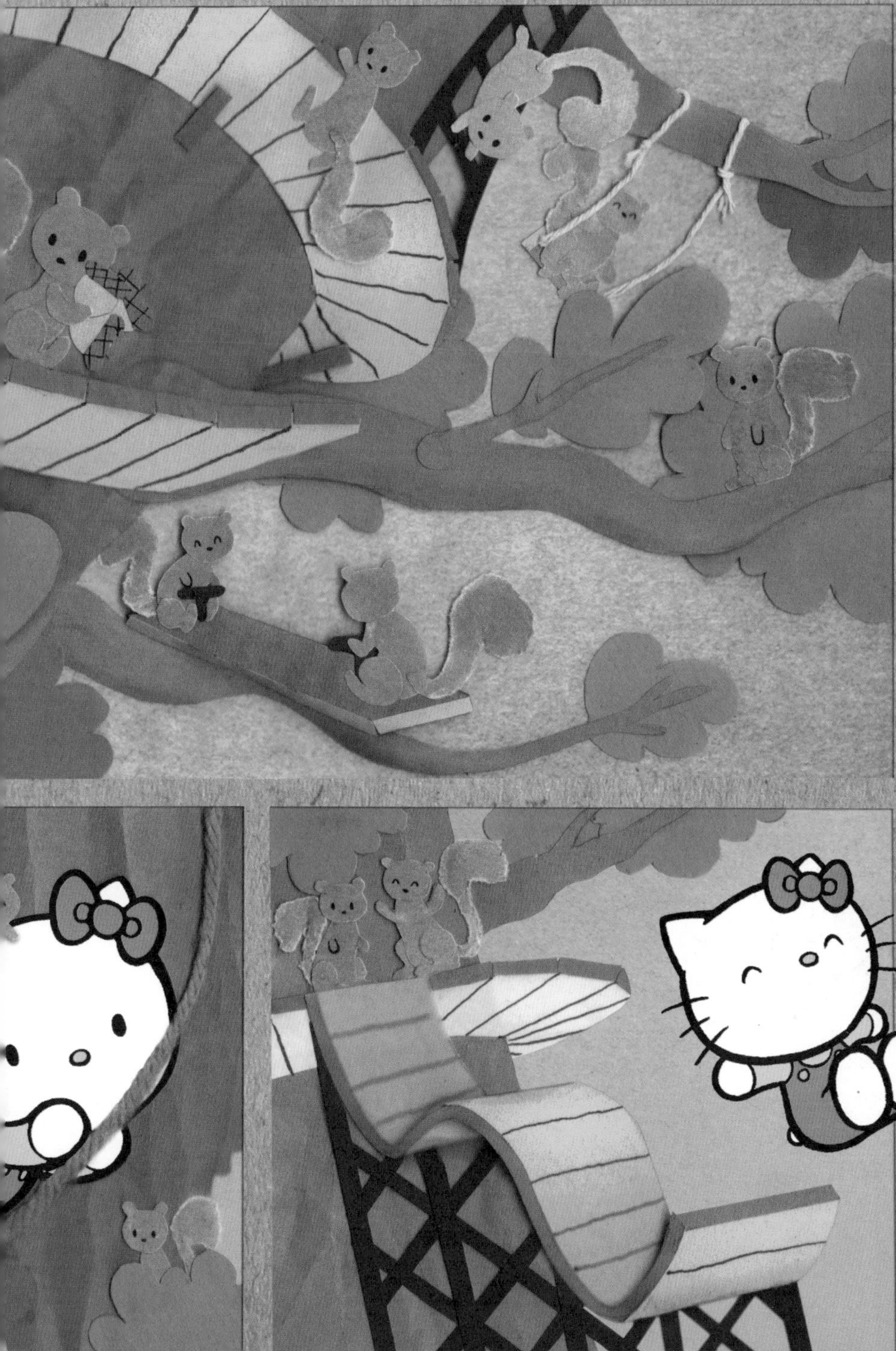

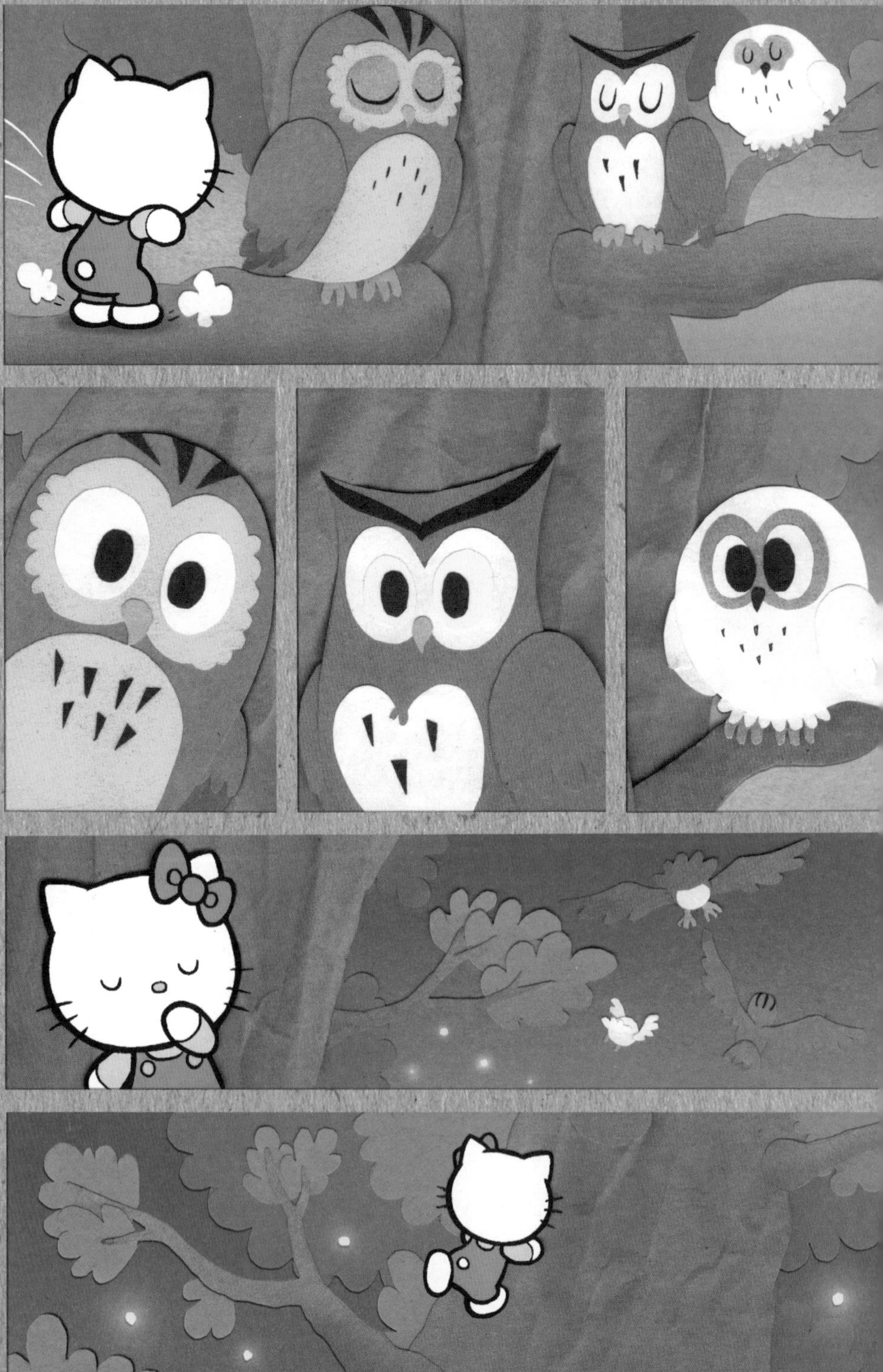

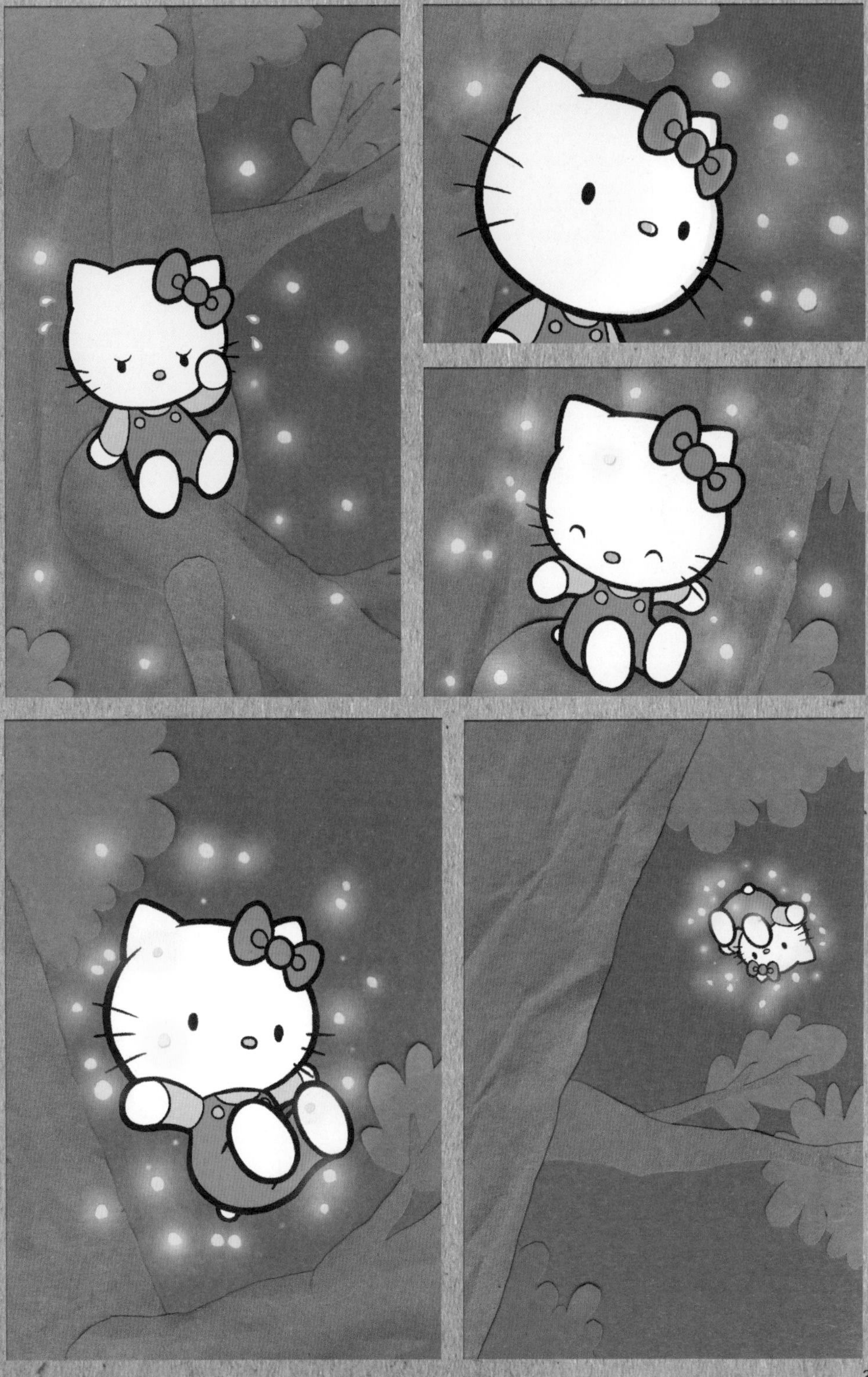

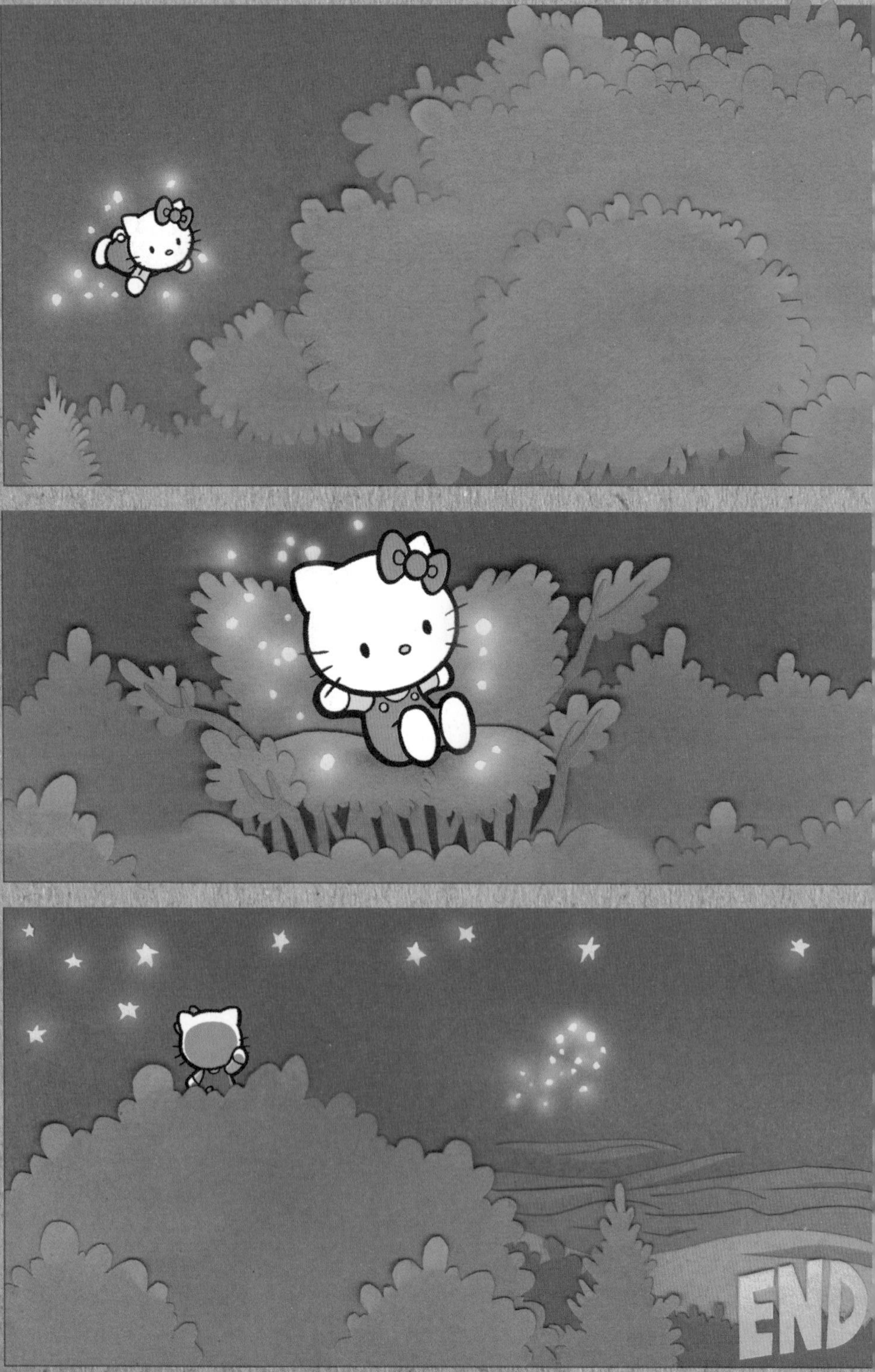
END

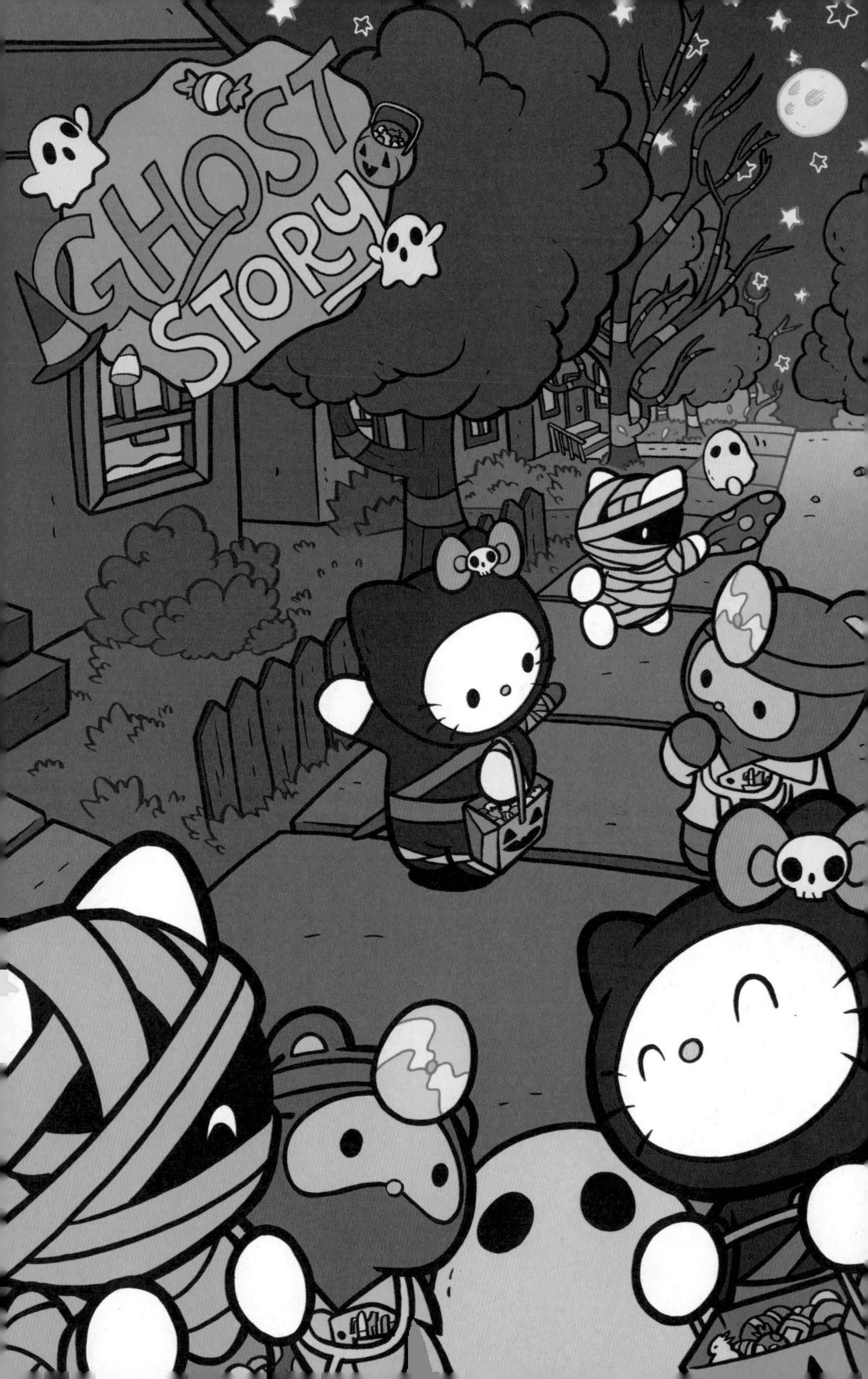
GHOST
STORY

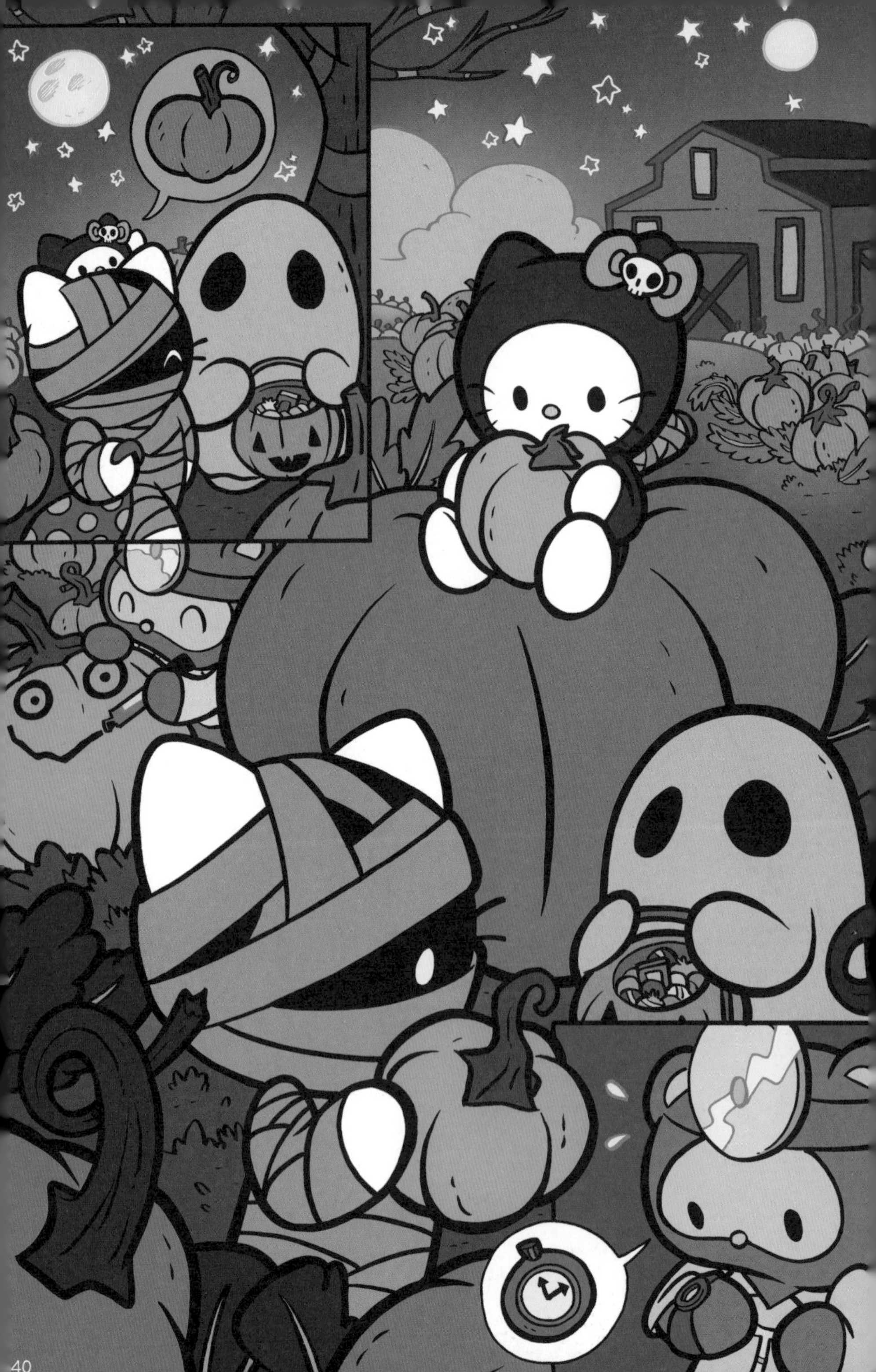

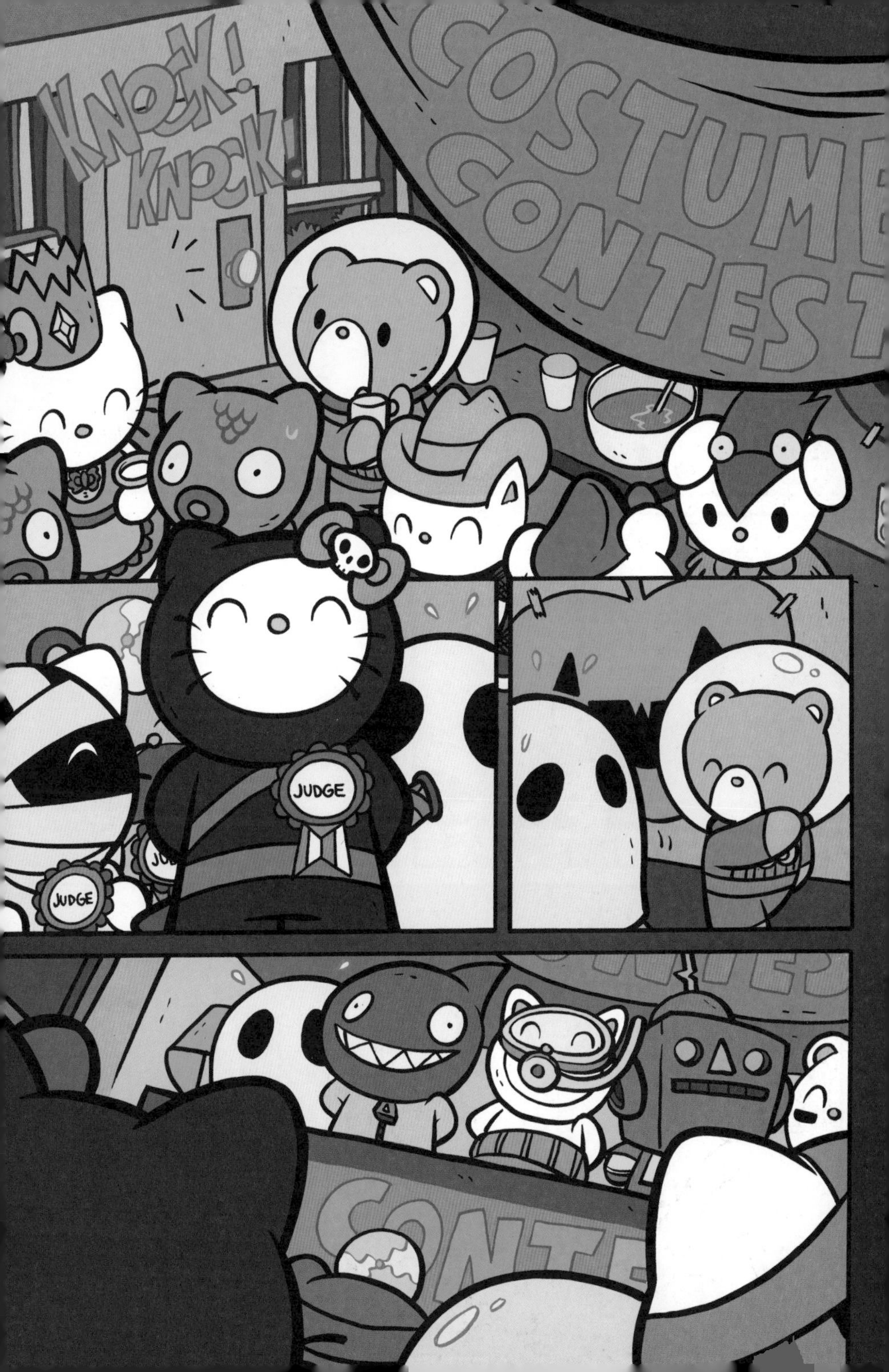
KNOCK! KNOCK!
COSTUME CONTEST
JUDGE
JUDGE
JUDGE

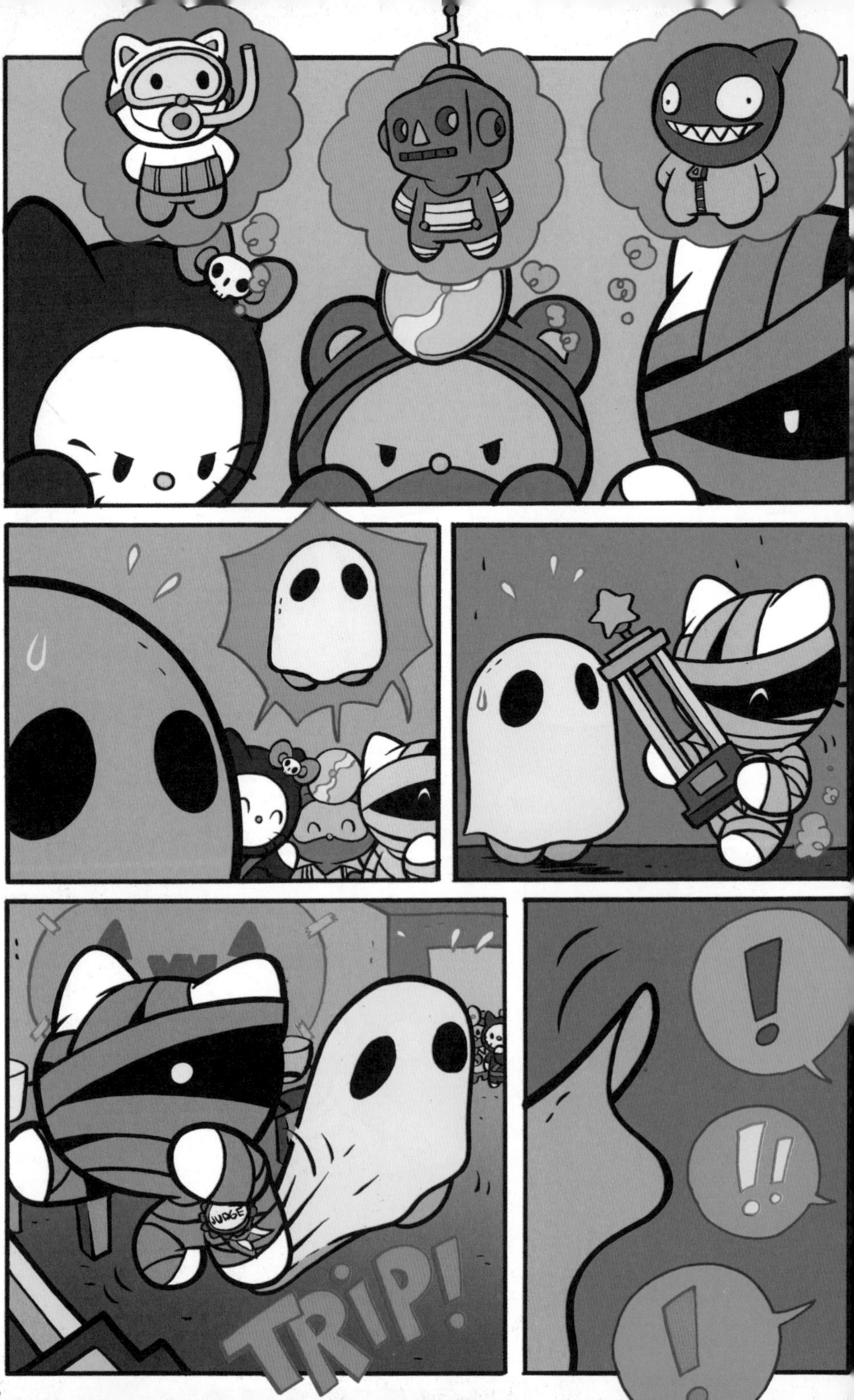
JUDGE
TRIP!
!
!!
!

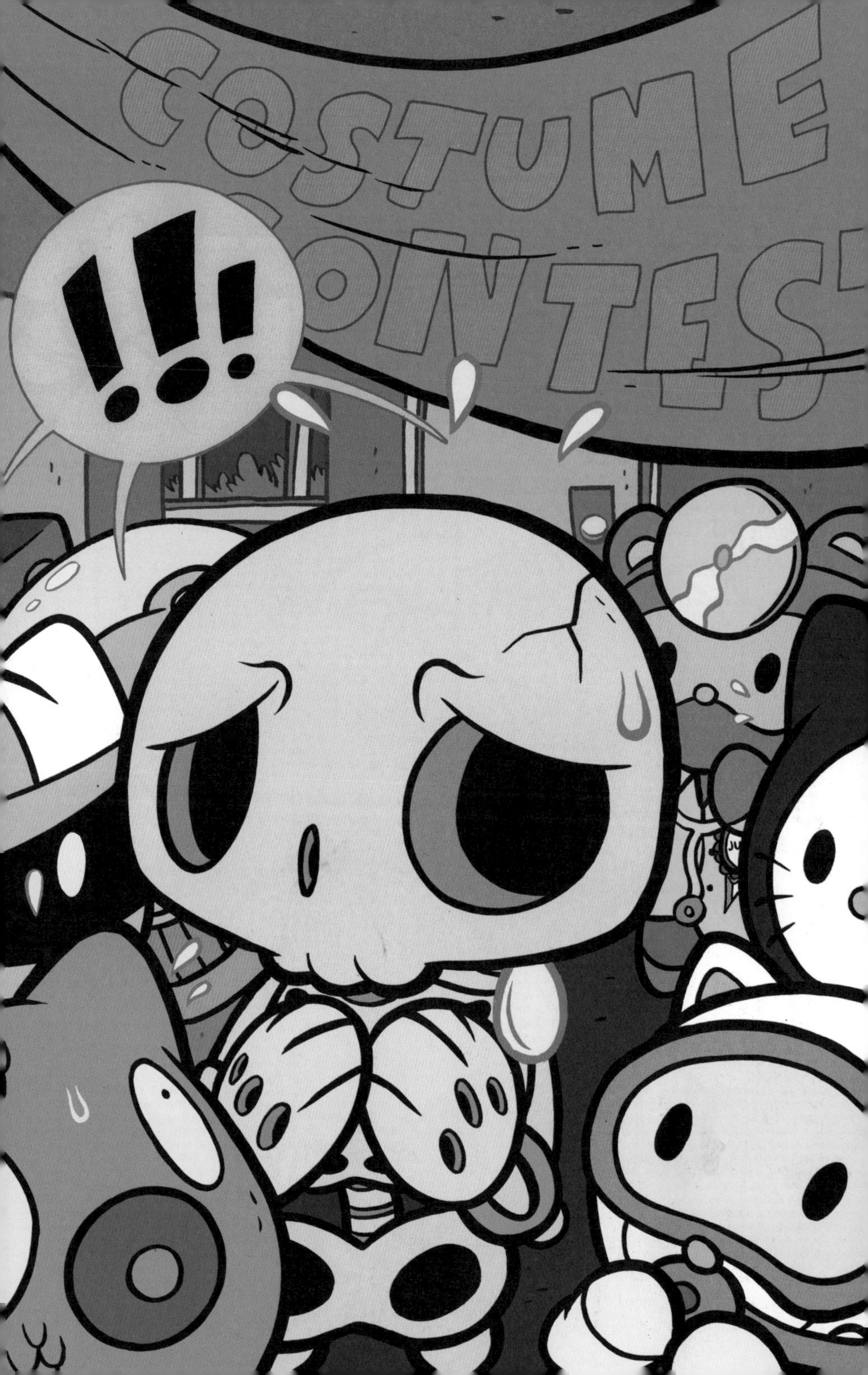
!!!
COSTUME

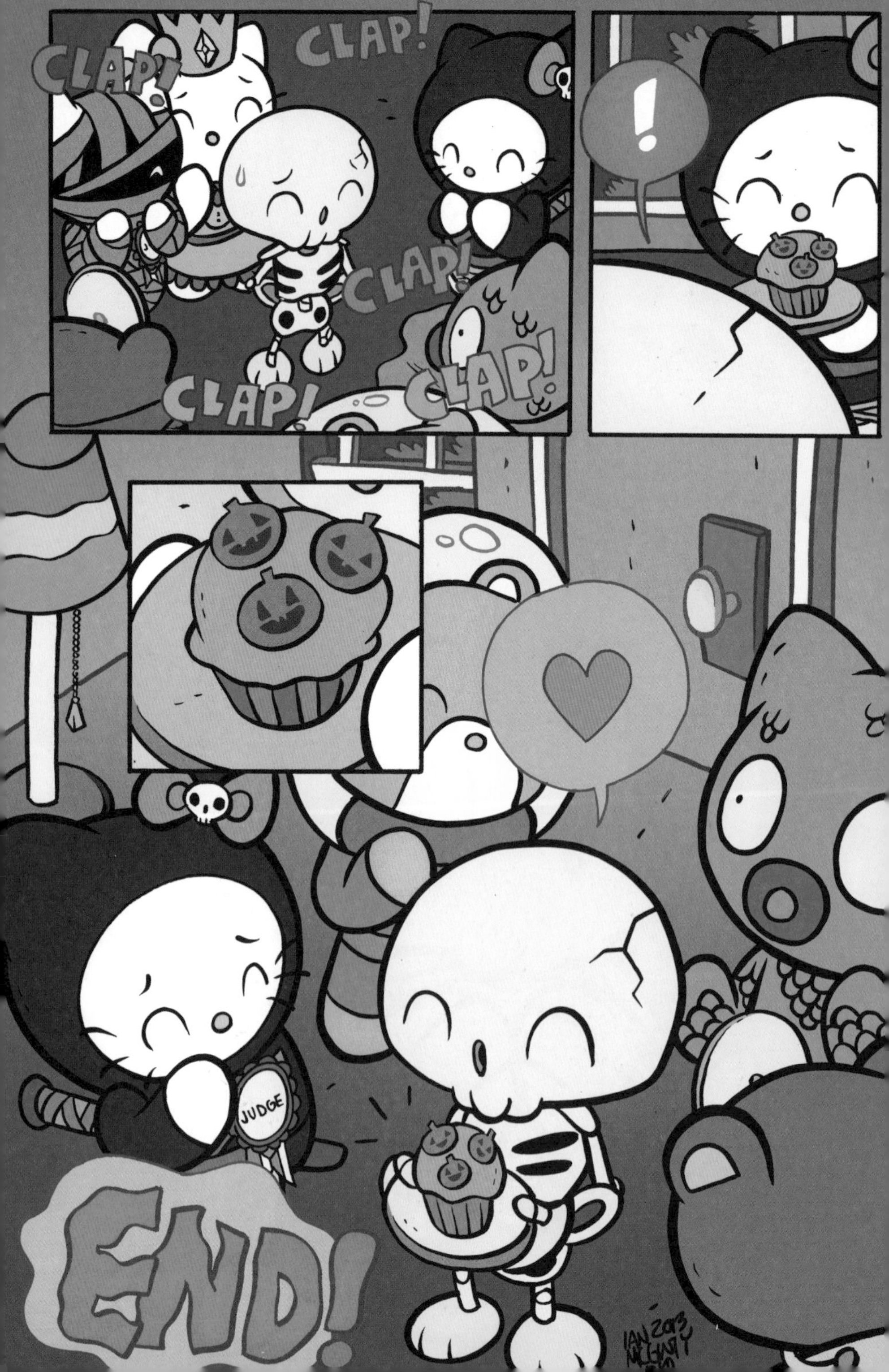
CLAP!
CLAP!
CLAP!
CLAP!
CLAP!
!
JUDGE
END!
IAN MCGINTY 2013

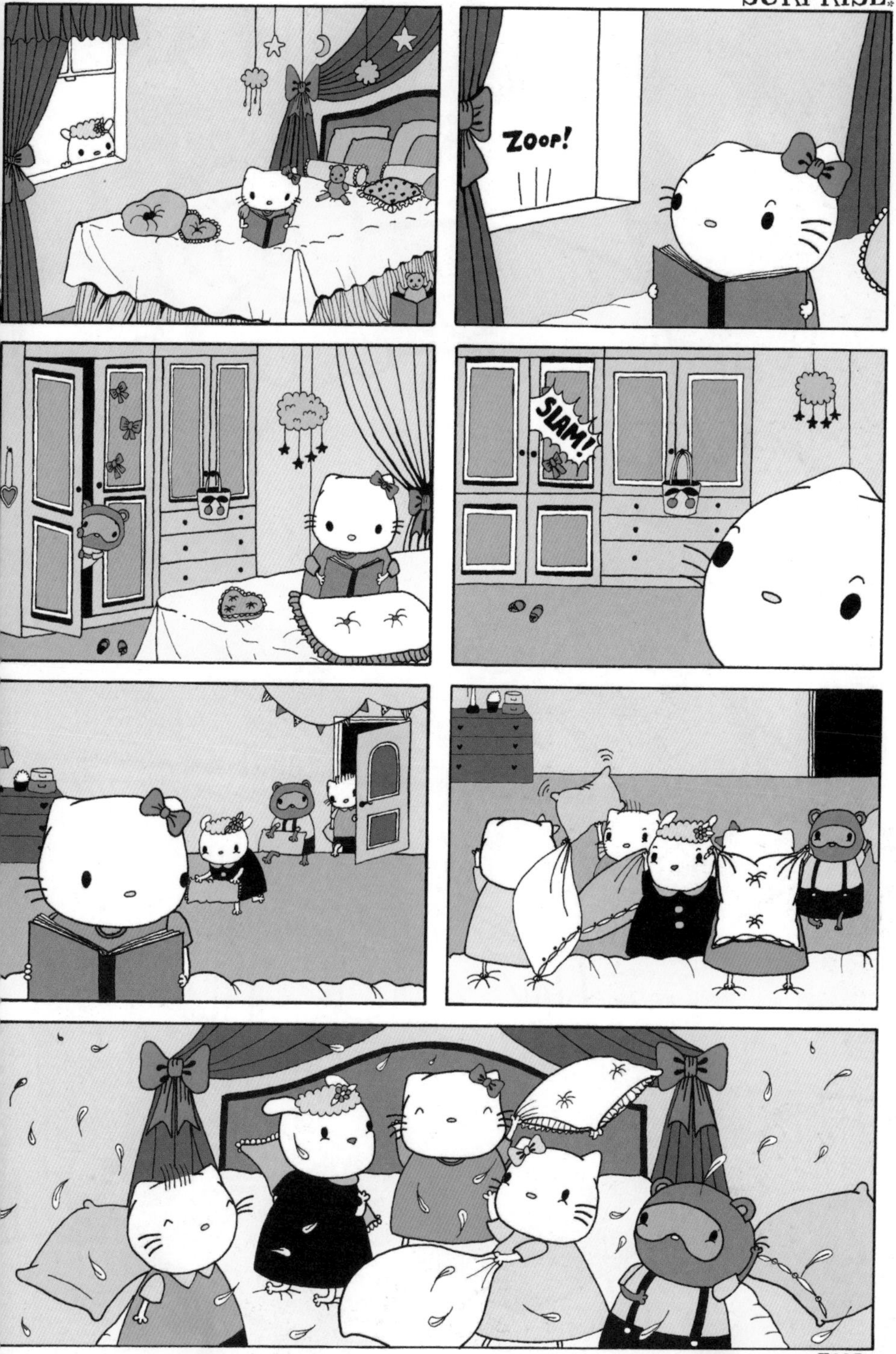
ZOOP!
SLAM!
END.

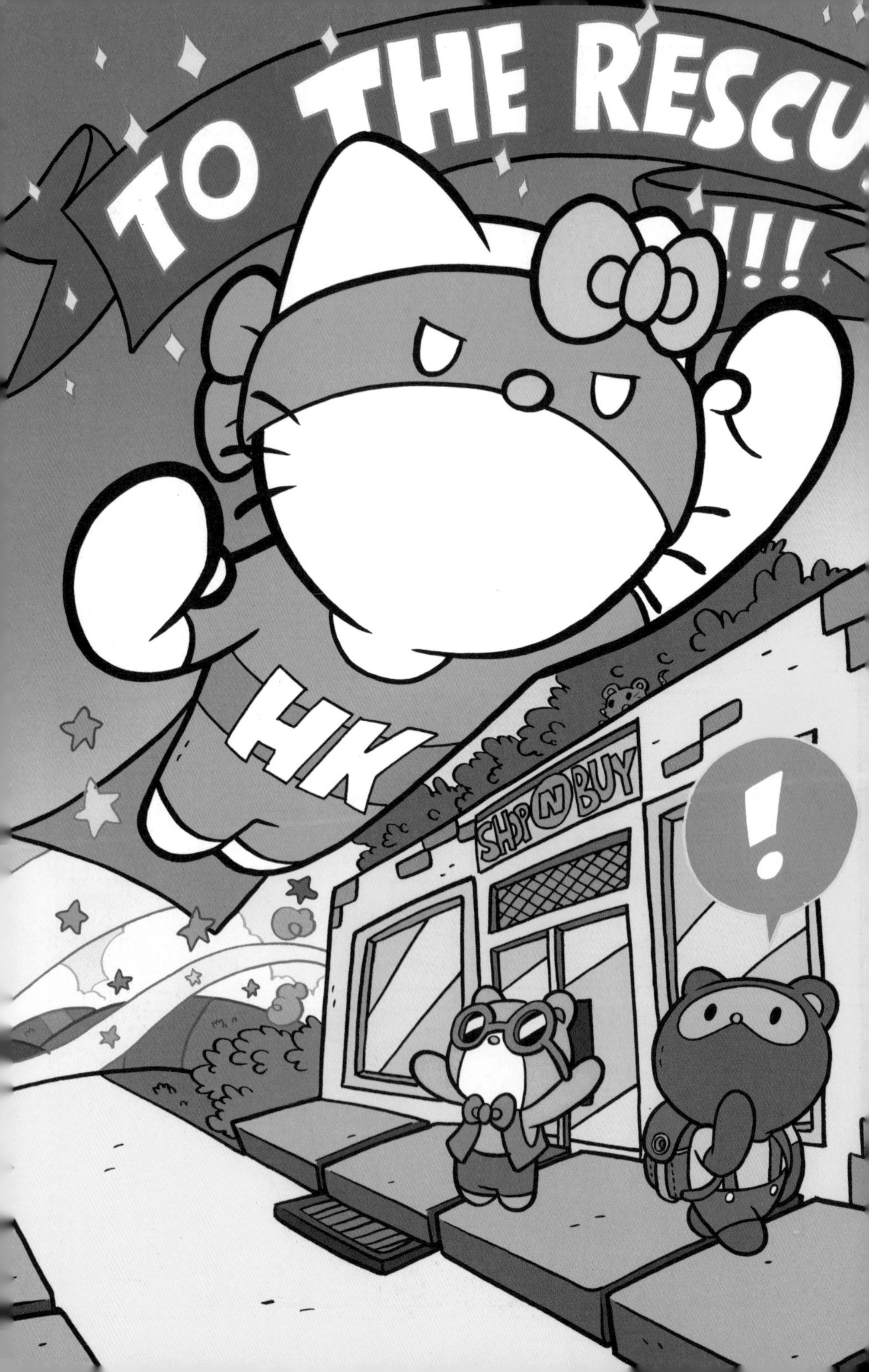
TO THE RESCU
!!
HK
SHOP N BUY
!

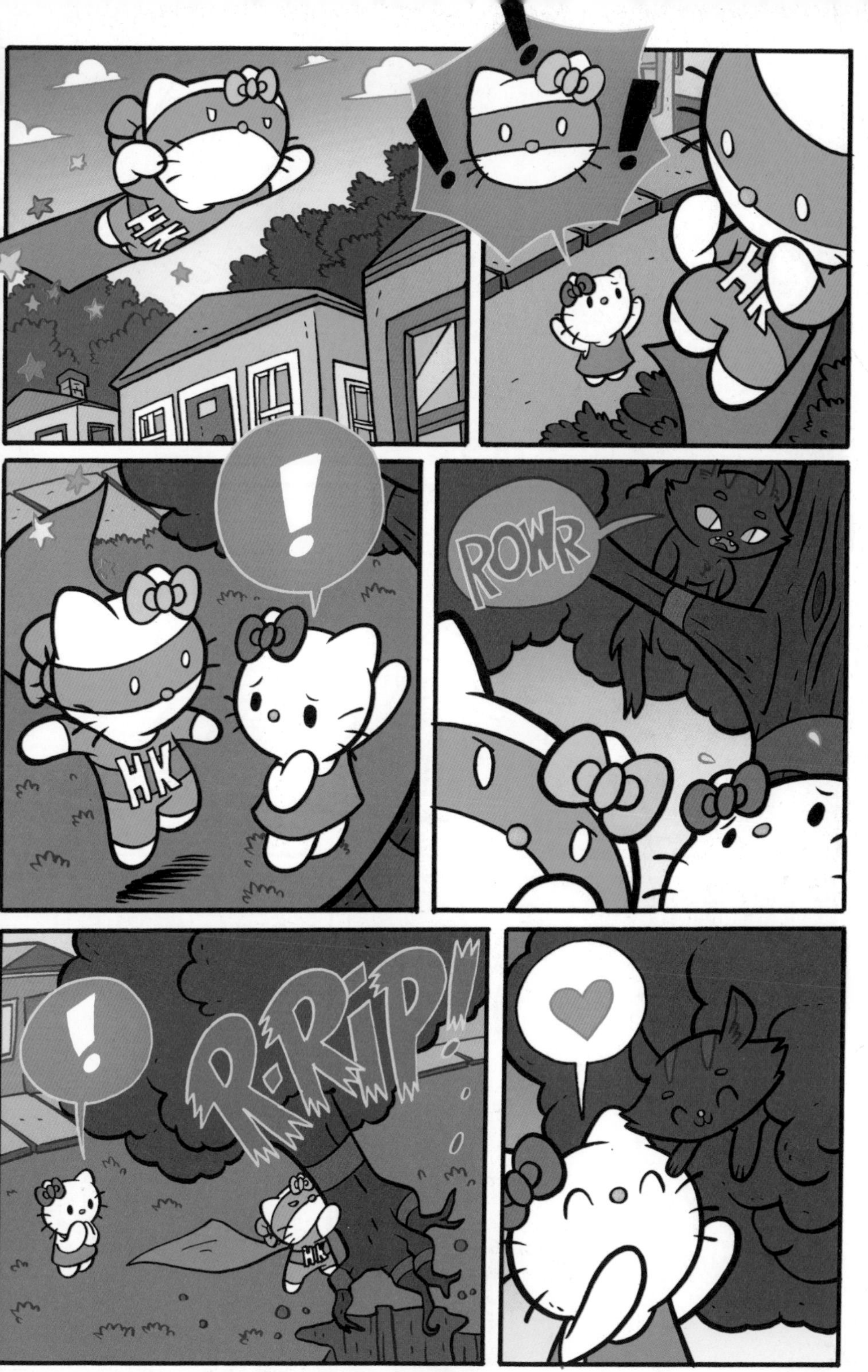

!
!
!
!
ROWR
!
R-RIP!

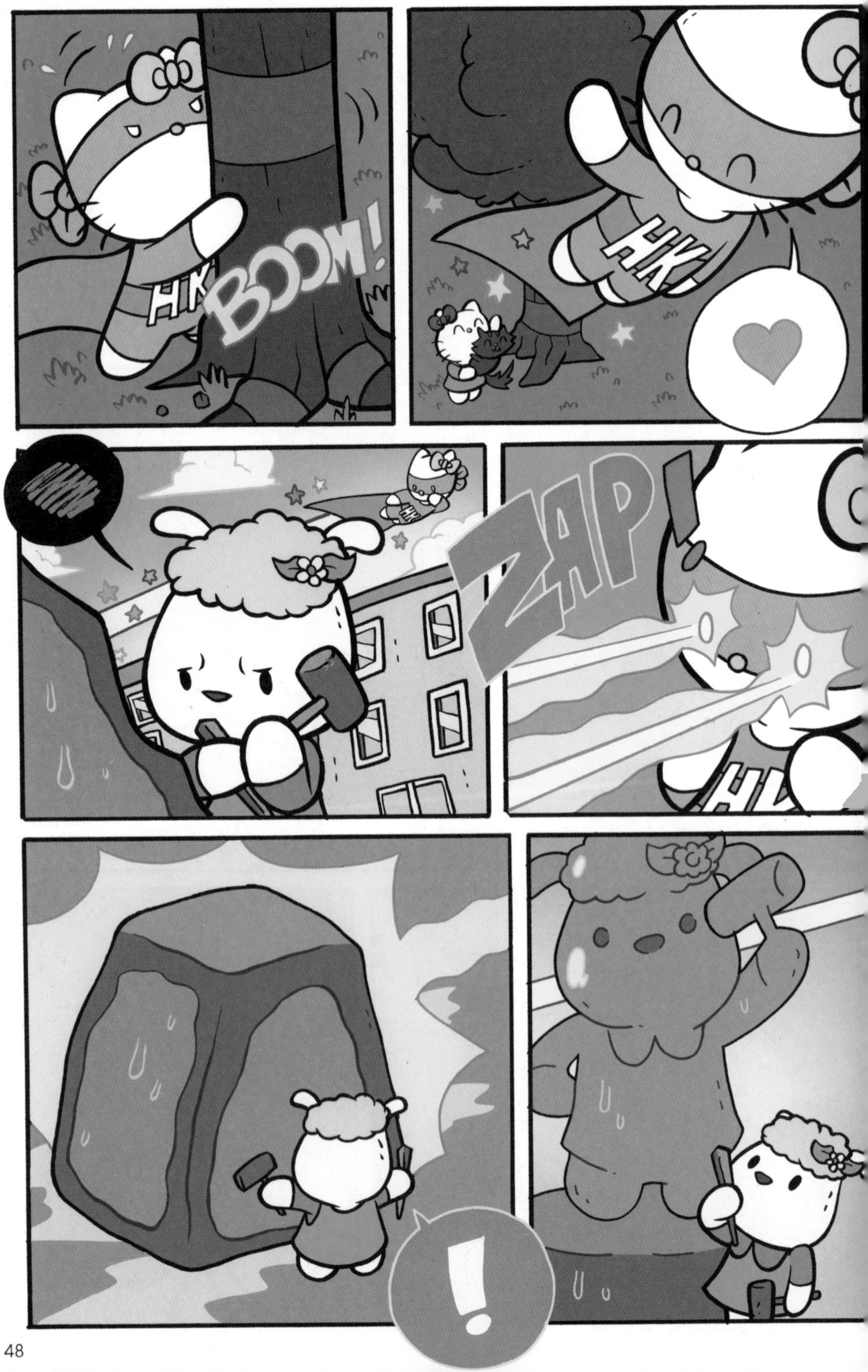
BOOM!
ZAP!
!

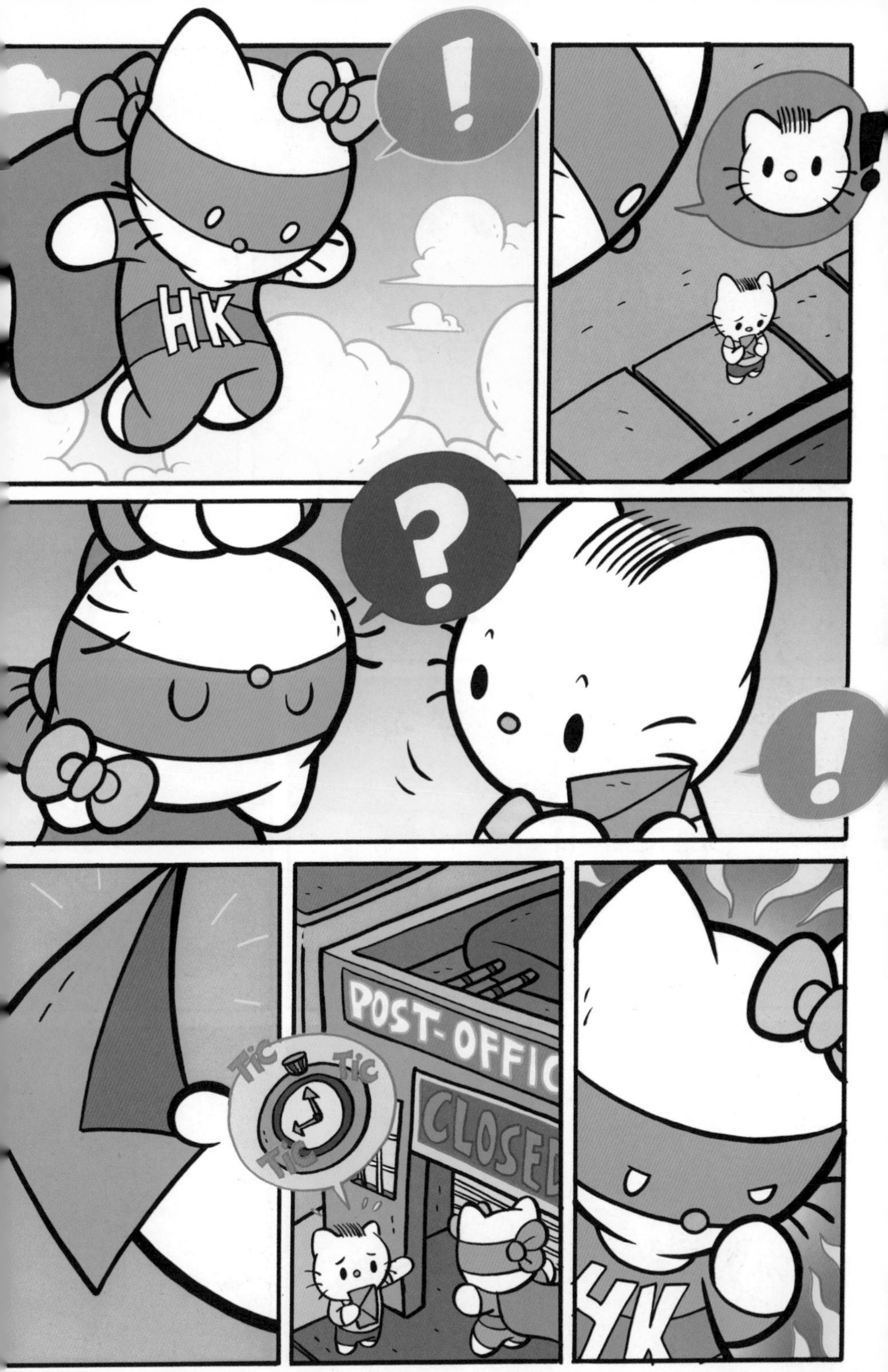
!
!
?
!
POST-OFFIC
CLOSED
TiC TiC TiC
HK
YK

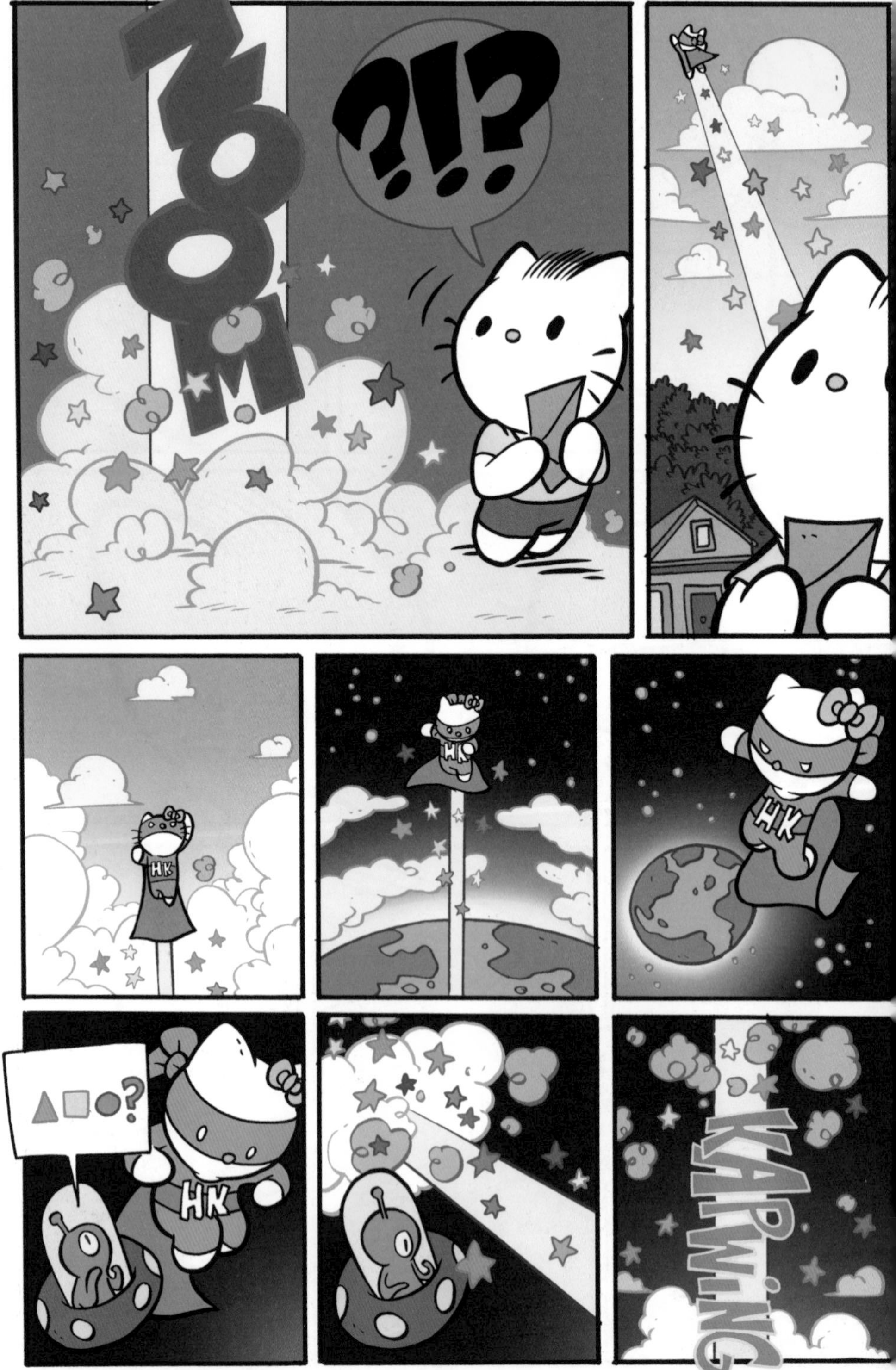
ZOOM
?!?
KAPWING!

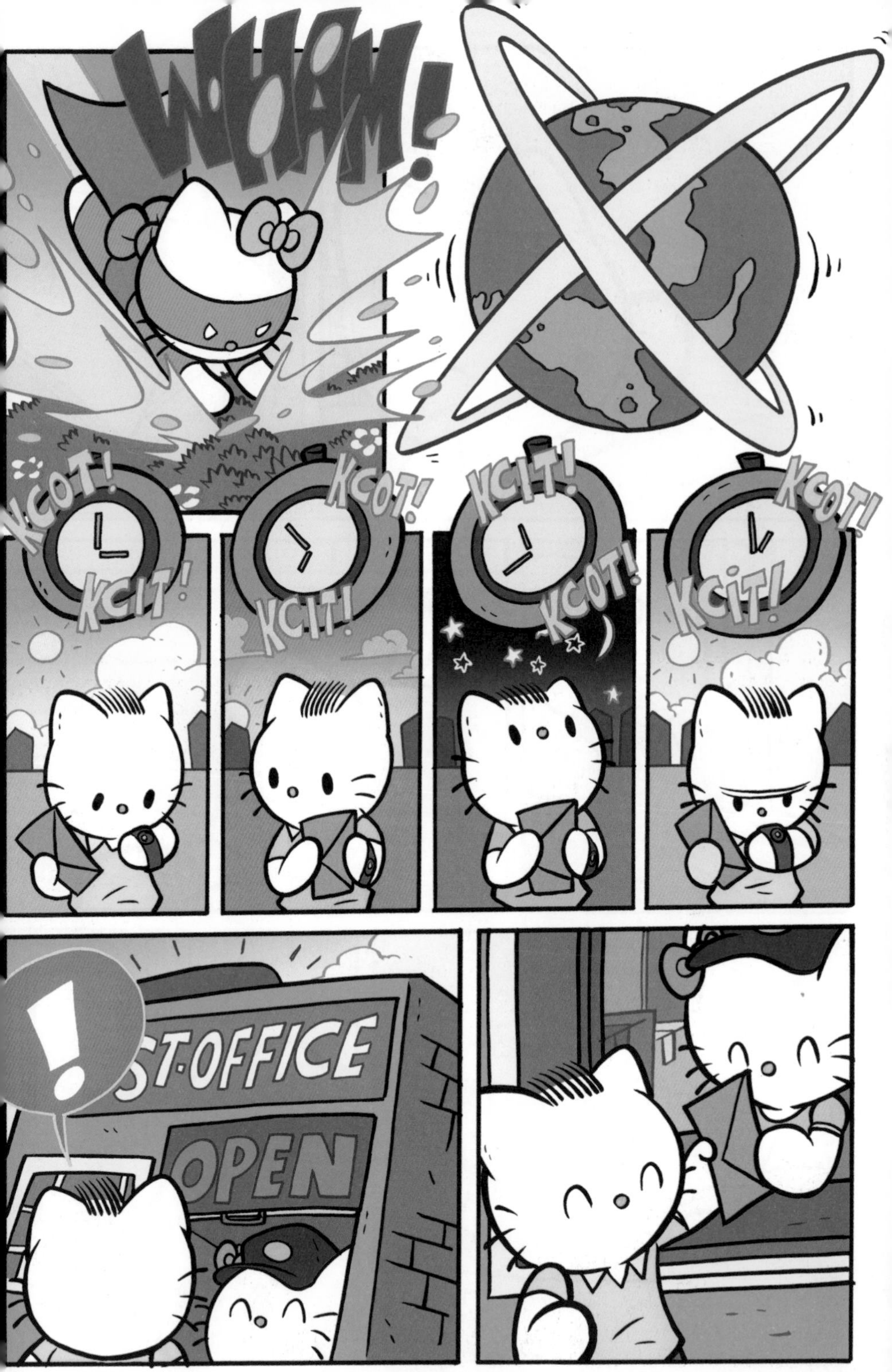
WHAM!
KCOT!
KCIT!
KCOT!
KCIT!
KCIT!
KCOT!
KCOT!
KCIT!
!
ST·OFFICE
OPEN

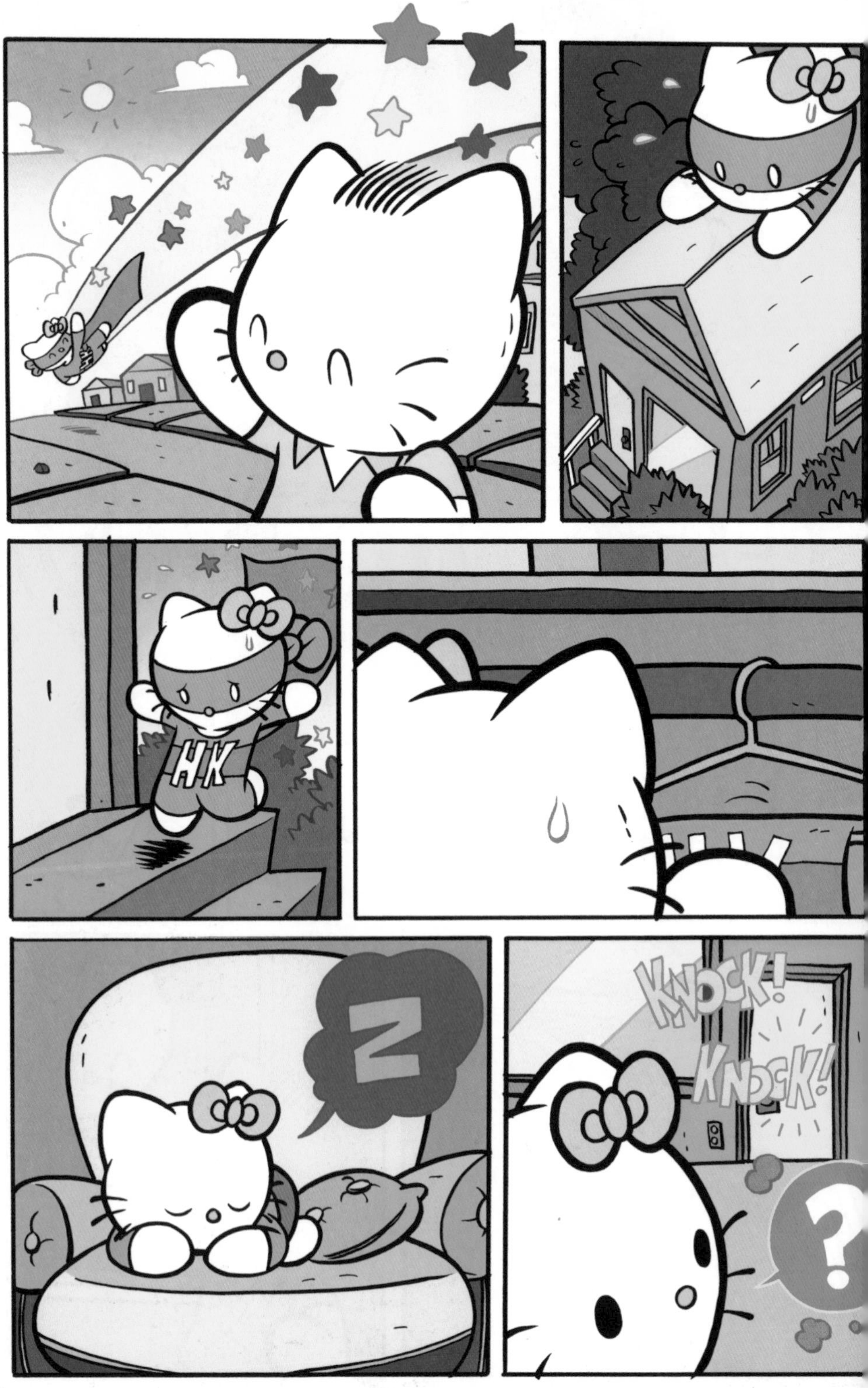
Z
KNOCK!
KNOCK!
?

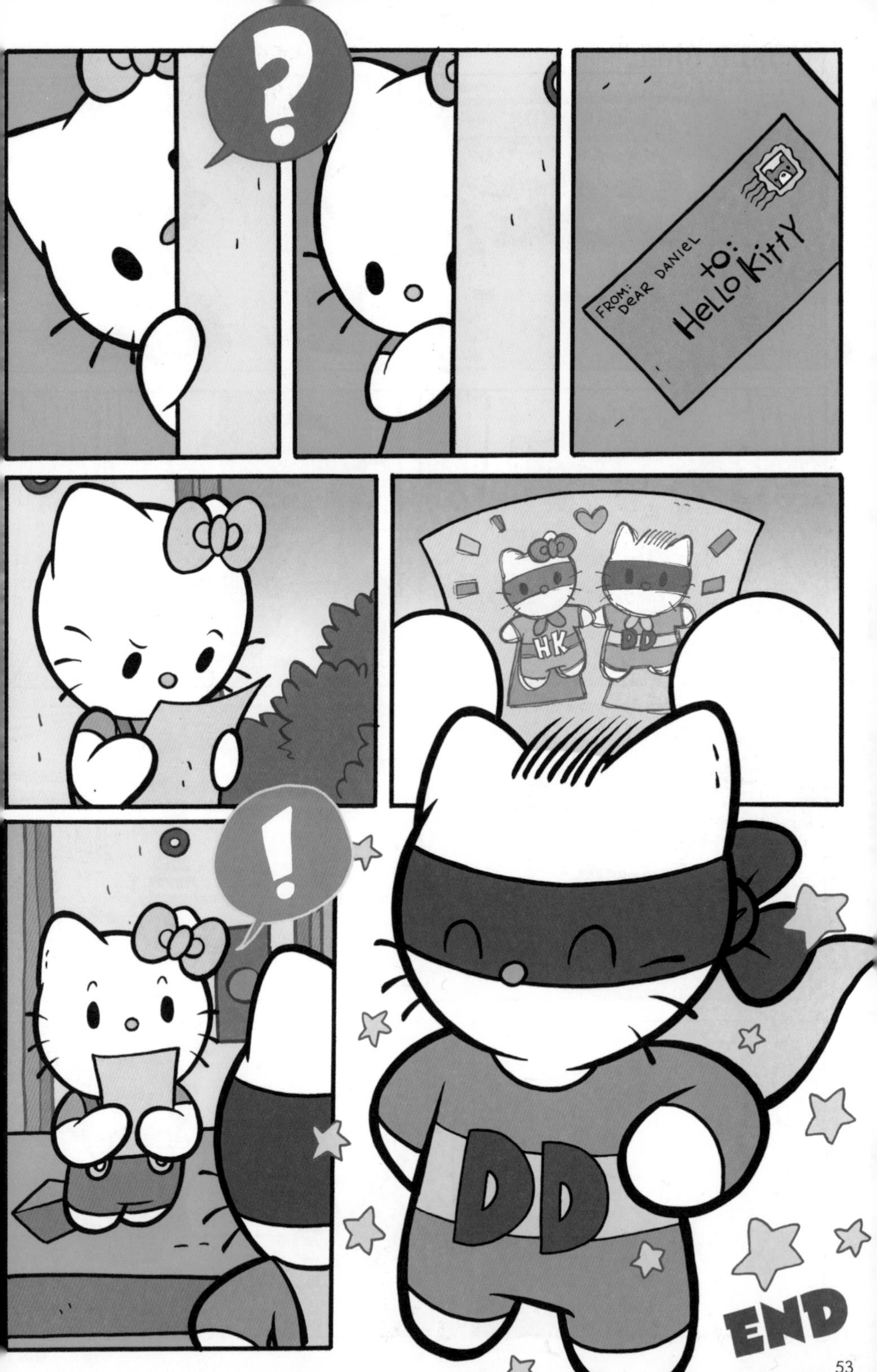
?
FROM: DEAR DANIEL
to: Hello Kitty
HK
DD
!
DD
END

MASKED BALL.

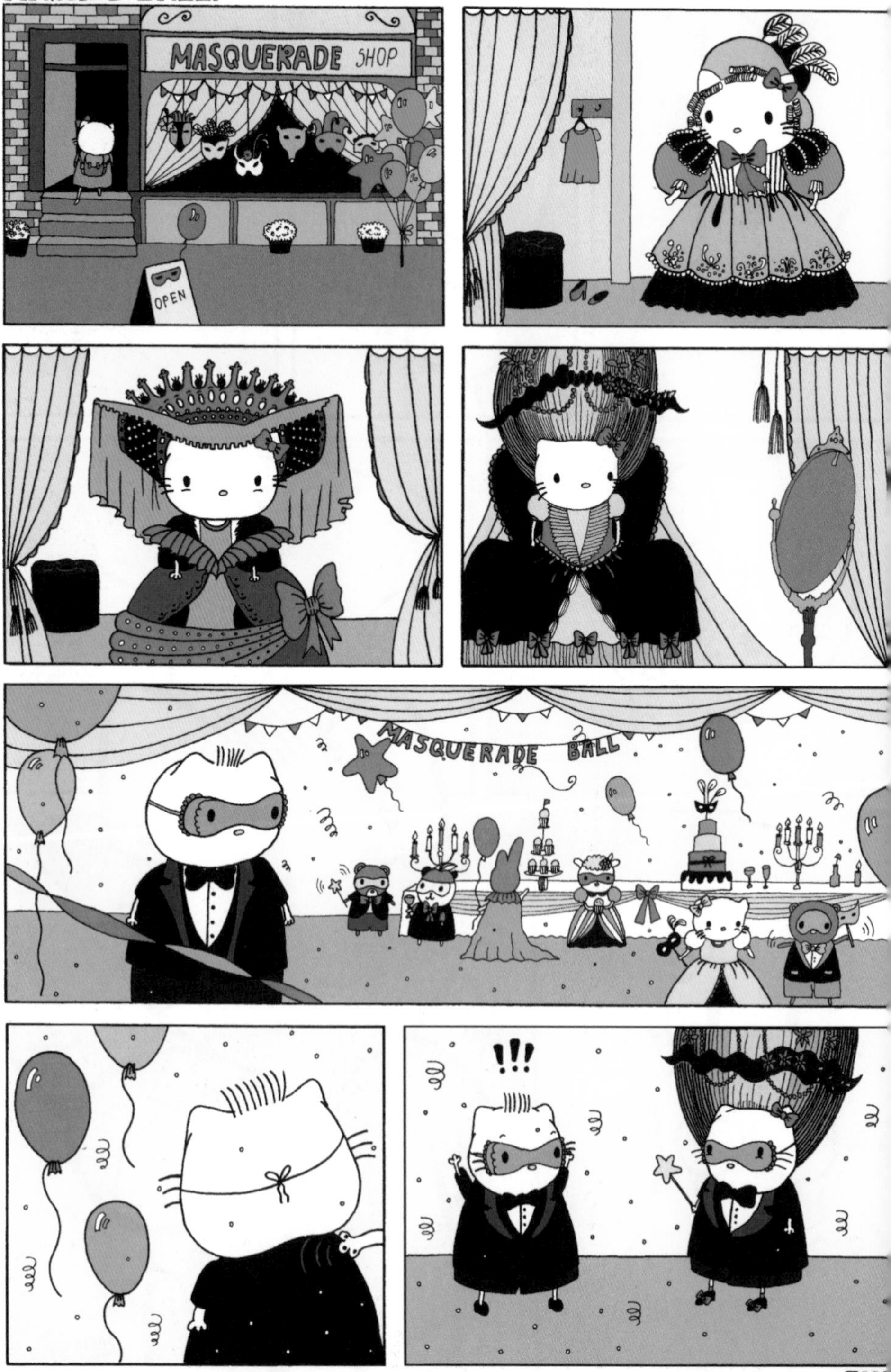
MASQUERADE SHOP
OPEN
MASQUERADE BALL
!!!

EN

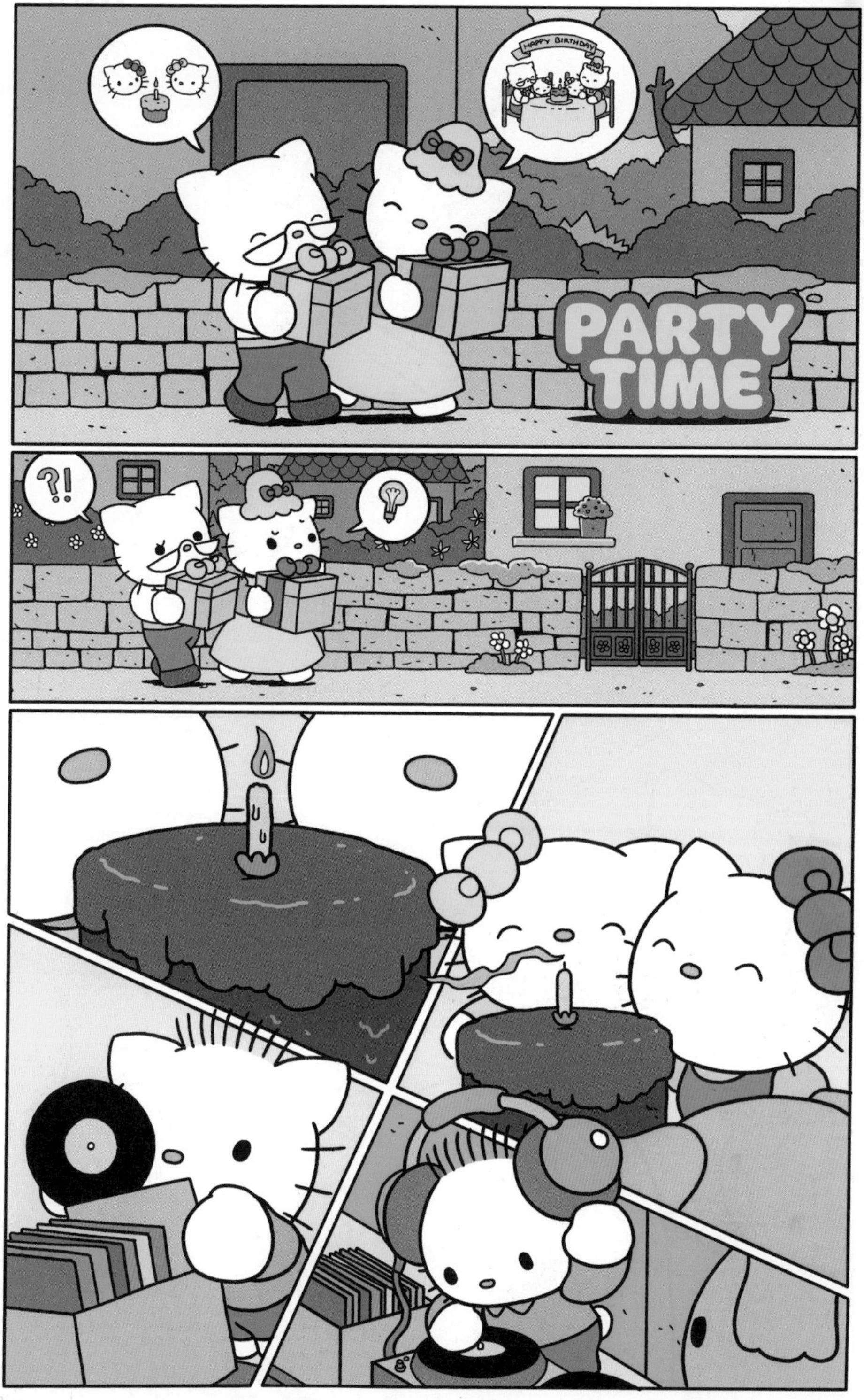
HAPPY BIRTHDAY
PARTY TIME
?!

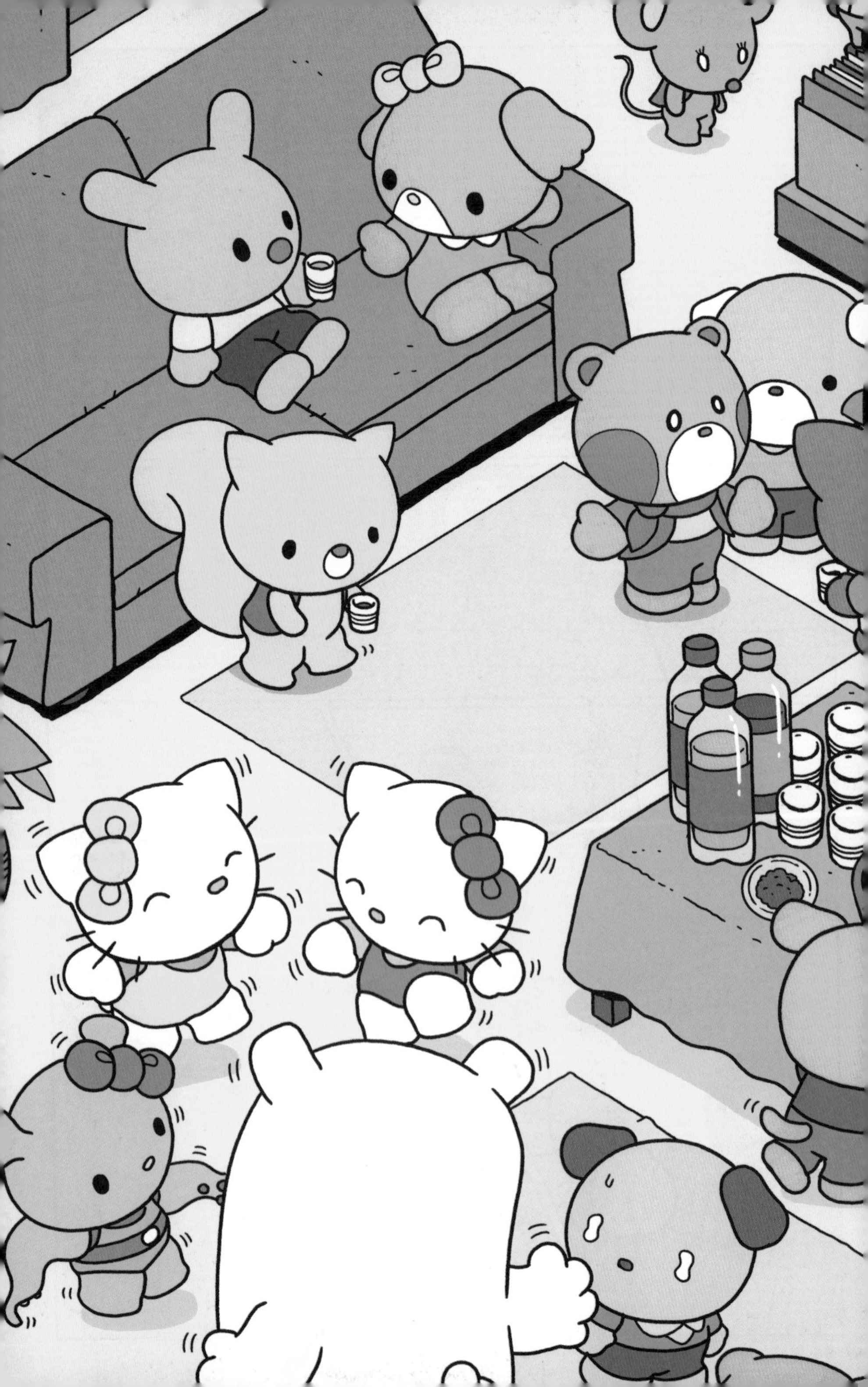

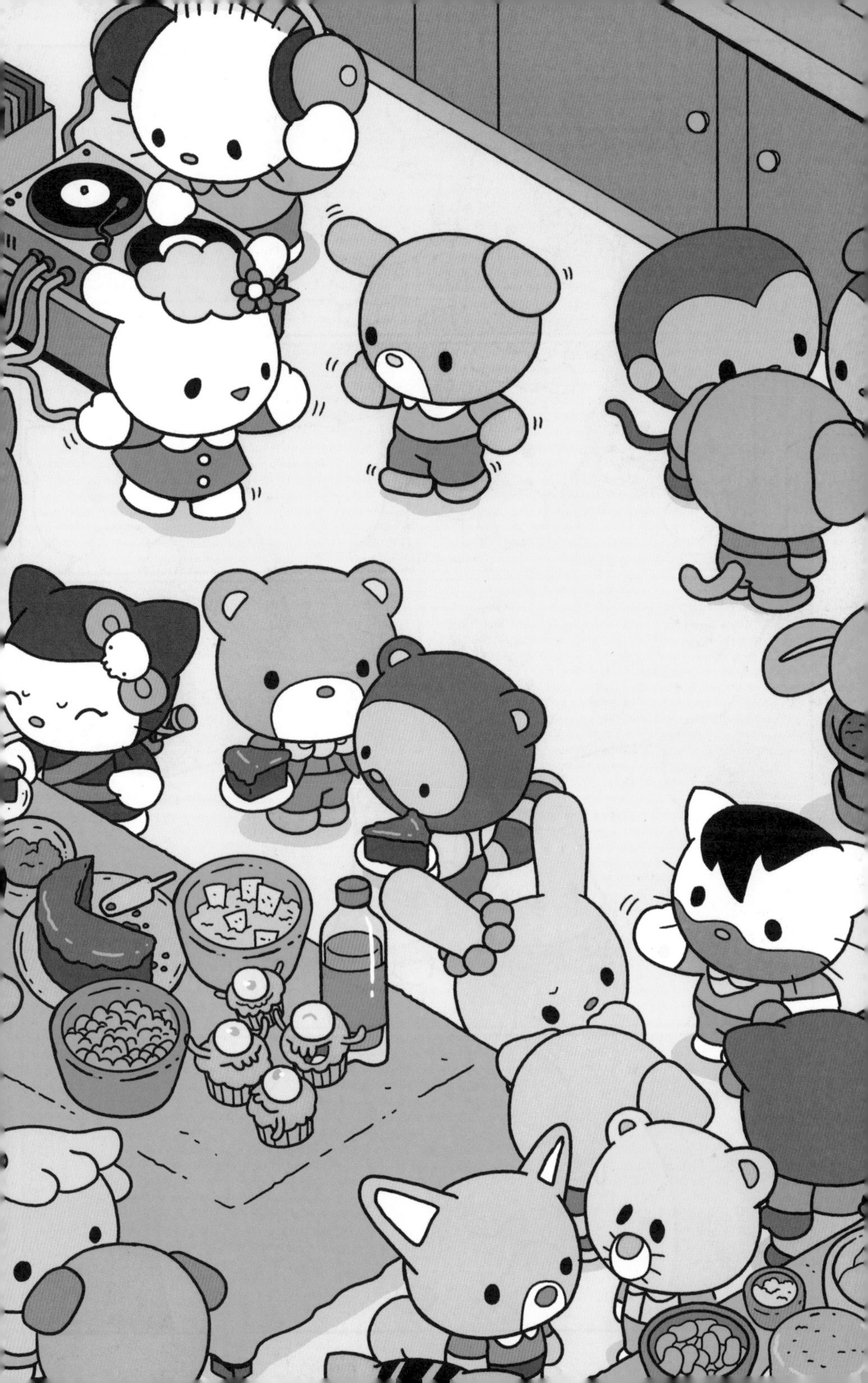

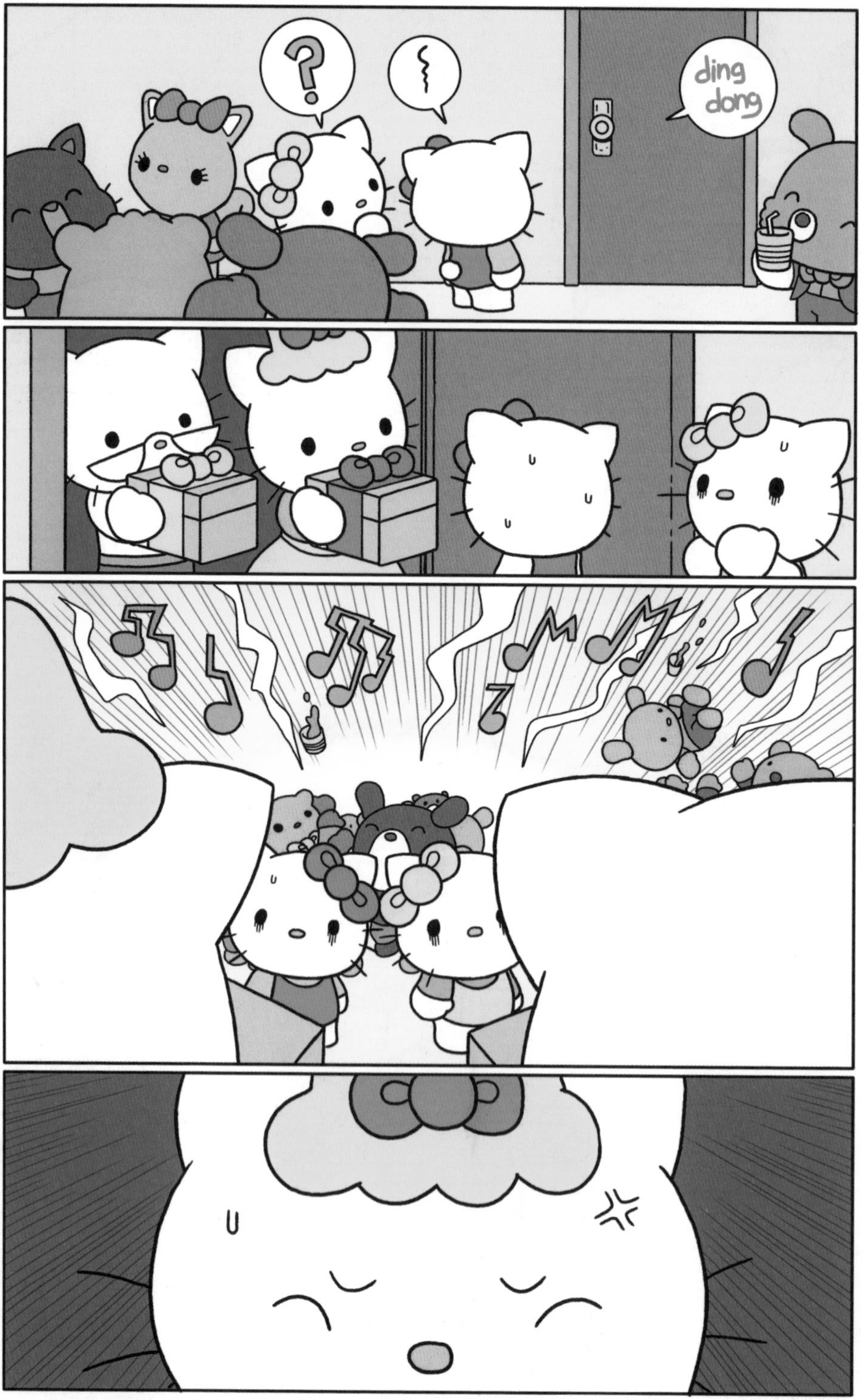
?
ding dong

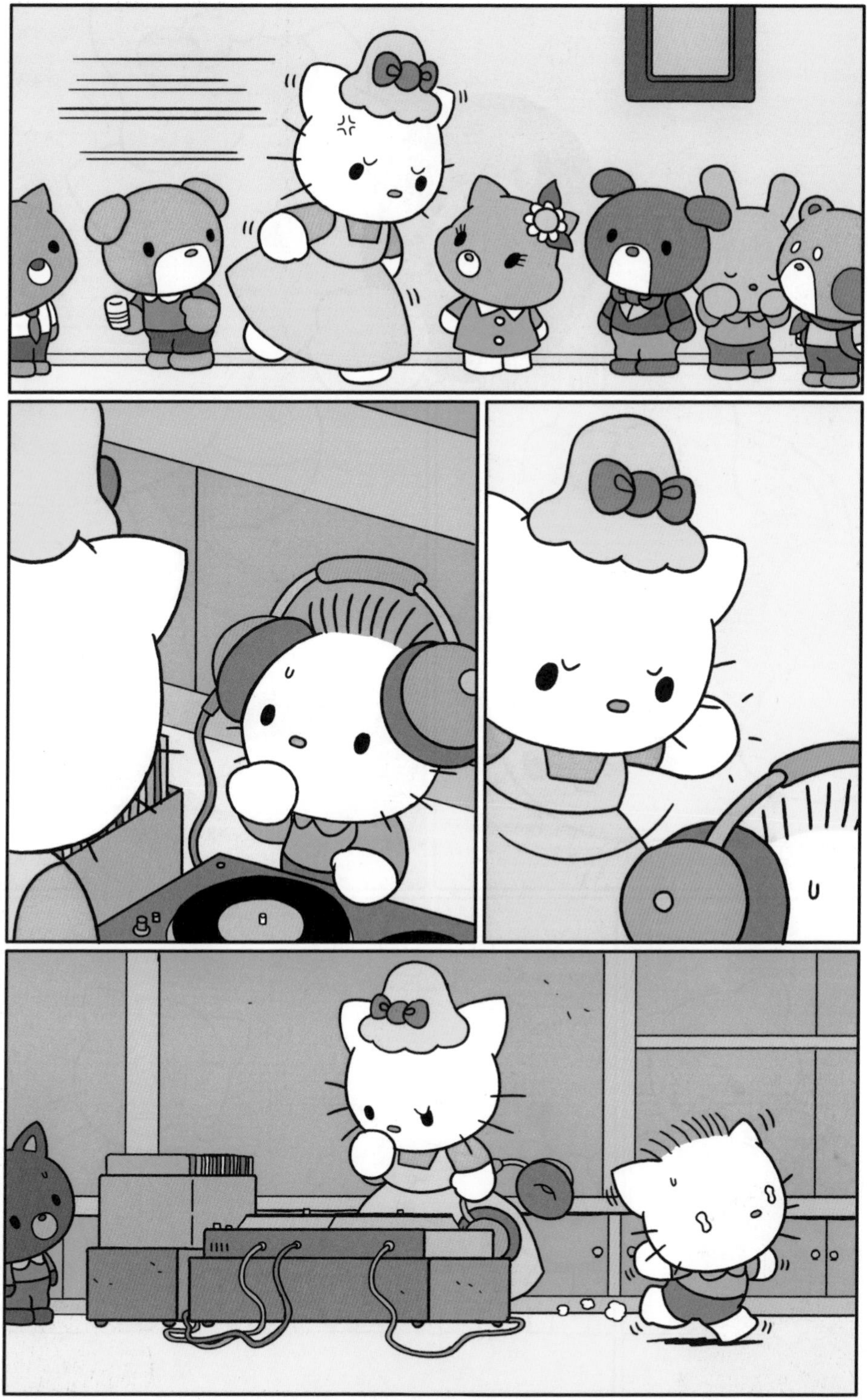

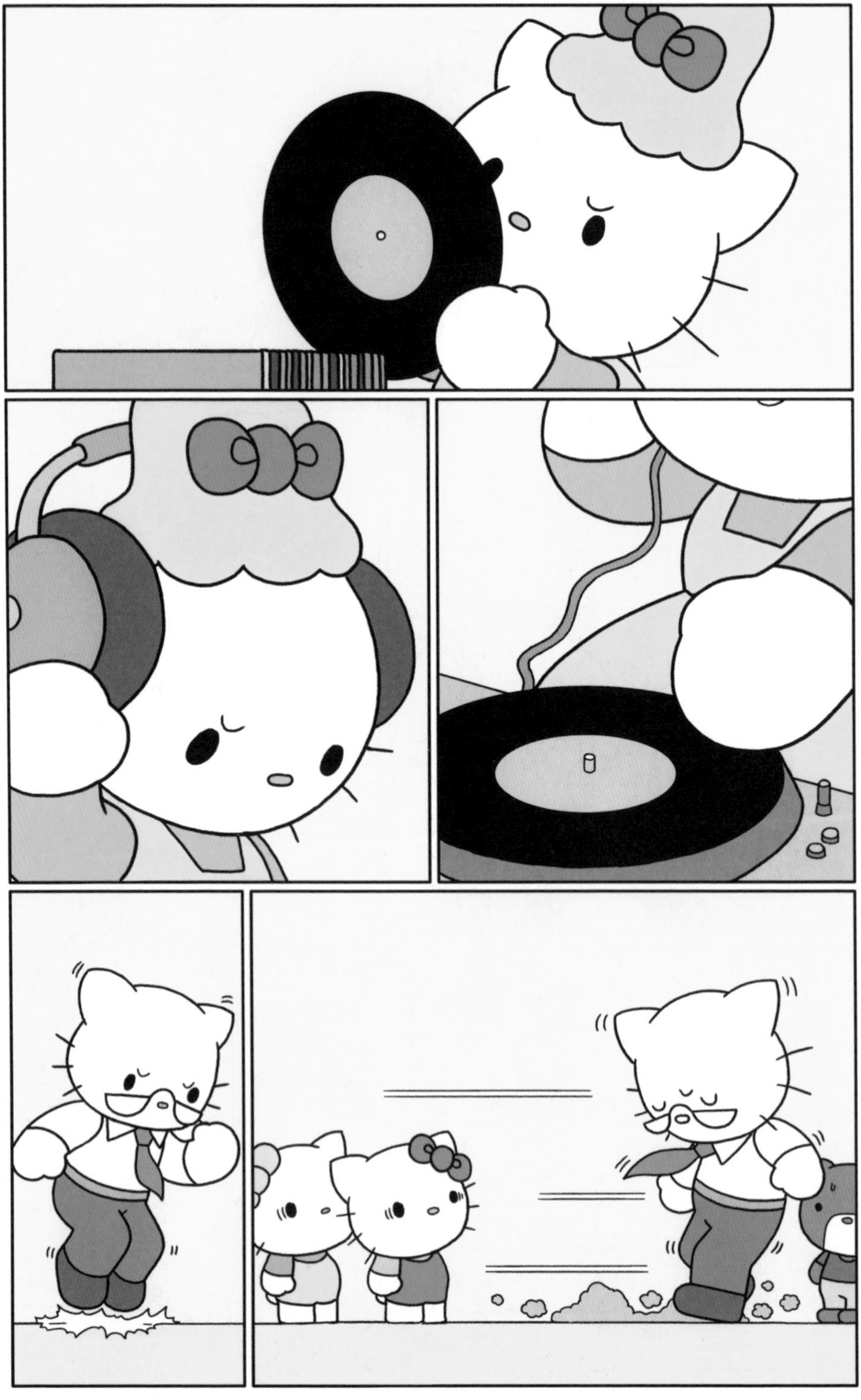

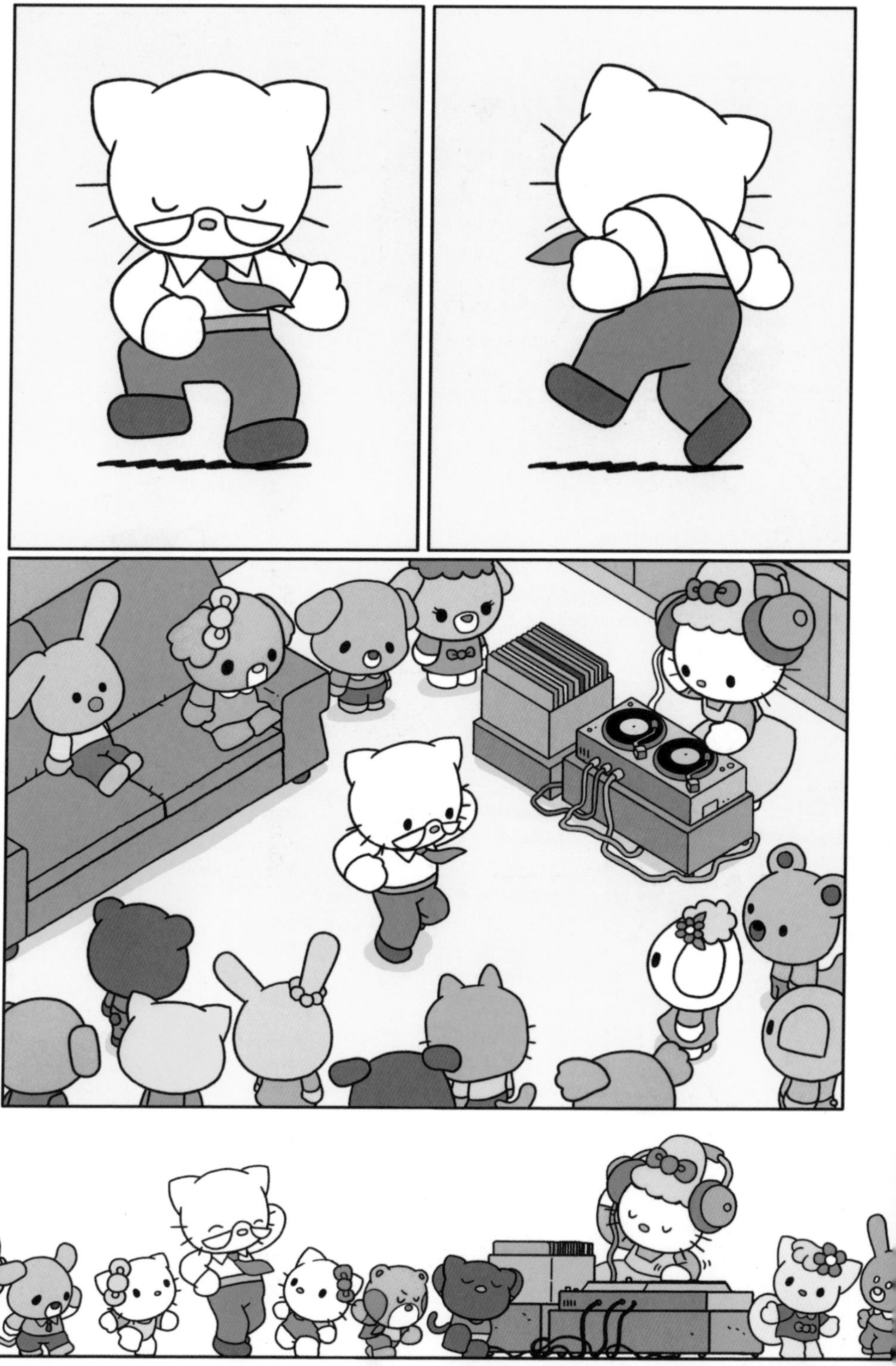

END

Creators

Jacob Chabot is a New York City-based cartoonist and illustrator. His comics have appeared in publications such as *Nickelodeon Magazine*, *Mad Magazine*, *Spongebob Comics*, and various Marvel titles. He also illustrated *Voltron Force: Shelter from the Storm* and *Voltron Force: True Colors* for VIZ Media. His comic *The Mighty Skullboy Army* is published through Dark Horse and in 2008 was nominated for an Eisner Award for Best Book for Teens.

Jorge Monlongo makes comic books, editorial and children's illustrations and video game designs and paints on canvas and walls. He combines traditional and digital techniques to create worlds in beautiful colors that usually hide terrible secrets. You can see his works in the press (*El Pais*, *Muy interesante*, *Rolling Stone*) and read his comic book series, *Mameshiba*, published by VIZ Media in the USA.

Ian McGinty lives in Savannah, Georgia, and also parts of the universe! Also, Earth. When he isn't drawing comics and rad pictures of octopuses (octopi?), he's laughing at funny-looking dogs and making low-carb burritos! Ian draws stuff for VIZ Media, Top Shelf Productions, BOOM! Studios, Zenescope and many more cool folk! But he cannot draw garbage trucks for some reason.

Anastassia Neislotova is a happy artist and children's book illustrator. She spends all her time creating nice illustrations and paintings, where she puts all her love and kindness. She loves making people smile. She feels very happy when her art can provoke positive emotions in people, and for this she is ready to draw forever. She also feels happy when feeding squirrels, stroking sausage dogs and eating up cream from cakes.

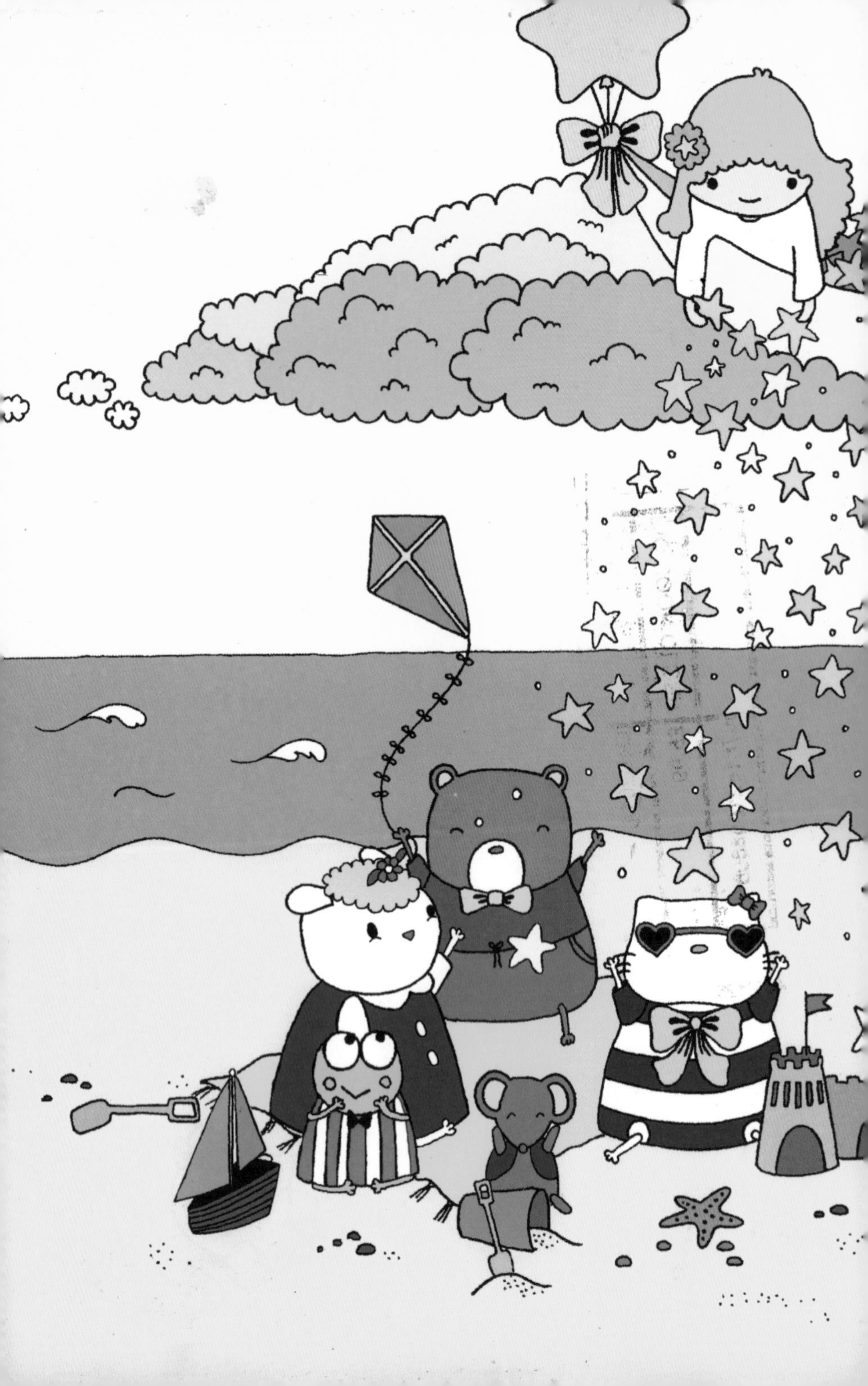